Life Long Lesson

R.Phillipson

*Dear Josie
Mucho love
x*

Life Long Lesson
Copyright Year:
© 2021
ISBN: 9781716860515
Imprint: LULU Independently published
First Edition
Language: English
Country: United Kingdom
Keywords: Fiction, Student, Teacher, Relationships, LGBT
License: Standard Copyright License ©
Copy Editor and Proof-reader: Hannah Simpson
Book Cover Designer and Illustrator: Bex Bowman

All rights reserved. No part of this book may be reproduced, scanned or distributed in any printed or electronic form without prior written permission from the author.

This is a work of fiction. Any similarity between the characters and situations within it's pages, places or persons, living or dead, is unintentional and coincidental.

Author(s): R.Phillipson

Special mention to the incredibly talented Hannah Simpson, Jessica Toft and Bex Bowman for the constant support and guidance throughout this process. I could not have done it without you all.

Don't judge a book by it's cover.

CONTENTS

Prologue
Chapter 1:   4 Years Before…
Chapter 2:   Aftermath
Chapter 3:   Pushing Boundaries
Chapter 4:   Round Two
Chapter 5:   Isolation
Chapter 6:   The Head
Chapter 7:   Exams
Chapter 8:   School's Out
Chapter 9:   Summer Holidays
Chapter 10: Results Day
Chapter 11: Out Of Hours
Chapter 12: Sweet 16
Chapter 13: First Time
Chapter 14: A-levels
Chapter 15: Weekend Away
Chapter 16: Close Call
Chapter 17: Christmas
Chapter 18: New Friends
Chapter 19: Paranoia
Chapter 20: Love Conquers
Chapter 21: Home Truths
Chapter 22: Two Worlds Collide
Chapter 23: Brought Back To Reality
Chapter 24: Peace Of Mind
Chapter 25: End Of The Beginning
Chapter 26: The Here and Now

Prologue

There are no accidents in life. People were always going to find out one way or another. Everything comes full circle. I am grateful it happened sooner rather than later. You might think it's harsh of me to say, but no explanation I give you will satisfy you. I know and understand that you seek resolution and explanations because you're human. It's natural instinct. But one day, I hope you will understand. One day maybe everyone will understand, but by then it might be too late. People usually look back on their life with some regret. I'm making sure I never get to that point. To live and react in the moment is the best feeling. It makes you free.

Less than two years, that's how long it took for my life to change dramatically. For my whole world to crumble around me. I cannot tell you how to respond to what I did, how to feel towards the decisions that I made. But what I can try and do is to explain, to try and make you understand, even if it's just a little bit, why I did what I did. I'm not a murderer by the way, I don't go on to tell you how I killed someone or kidnapped someone, nothing like that. But it was bad, in the eyes of everyone around me. It was the worst thing I could've ever done.
But I knew. I always knew.

So, since I guess you're interested in what I've got to say, curious perhaps, I suppose then I should introduce myself to you. My name is Maxine Ann Watts. I am nineteen years old and I live on the outskirts of

Manchester. I live in a nice, modern, three-bed detached house. It's got it's own drive and a big back garden. I have lived there for nearly two years now. I work in retail part time and I've been doing an online fashion course. I finish the course in a few months and I'm hoping to get an entry level job in a fashion company.

  I don't really see anyone any more- family, friends. You could say I am alone; it feels that way sometimes. Not by choice, it's just that things are different now. I suppose I had a path to take, and some might think I took the wrong one. That's their opinion, and I'm sure you'll have yours by the end. That's okay. For the first time in so long, I feel at peace with my choices, my decisions, my life.

  I sat in a park this morning. I've been to that park a lot over the years, it helps me feel closer to someone. I usually sit in the same spot, a small picnic bench on one side of the hill. It's hidden by trees, away from everything else. I like sitting up there. It's peaceful, watching people from afar. They walk their dogs, play with their children, listen to the birds. When I went today it was busy with a family, so I had to go further into the park. I sat on a bench opposite the swings. Children were playing, screaming and laughing while their parents chatted over their morning coffee. A perfect picture of normal life.

  One girl caught my attention. She must have been around ten years old, with dark hair and pale skin. She had a bright blue coat on. She stood at the top of the slide and looked in my direction, and before she went down, she smiled at me. Such an innocent smile. I smiled back and admired her natural beauty and grace as she enjoyed the park. I wondered what her home life was like? Does she live with both her parents? Does she have brothers and sisters? Will she be popular at school? I wondered what she would want to be when she was older? Writer, nurse, teacher, model? The possibilities are endless. She has her whole life ahead of her, so many hopes and dreams. I remembered when I was that little girl running around, with no cares, no problems, no worries. Just young and free.

As I walked away from the park, I looked back. The little girl carried on playing, oblivious to me watching her. I wondered what would become of her? Would she make people proud? Would she turn out bad? I guess I will never know.

Present Day – 3.00PM Outside Down Lock Prison

It's a Saturday afternoon. I am standing in front of a tall barbed wire fence at *Down Lock Prison,* just outside of Manchester. It looks electrified. It is intimidating, the way it stands over me. It is the same fence I have walked past every day for the last 18 months. Only this time I don't walk past. I stop, and I wait. I am nervous, anxious, scared but also a little bit excited at the thought of a new start. I have tried to make an effort though. It's been so long since we last saw each other.

I have had my hair done, coloured dark brown and straight, long down my back. I have bought a new outfit for the occasion, black skinny jeans and a baggy blue jumper, with small black heel boots. I think it looks very grown up. I hope she likes it. I hope she thinks I look well. It's warm with a slight, much-wanted breeze. I have sunglasses on my head and I am clutching my hands. I can't stop fiddling with my silver bracelet. I love this bracelet. It was given to me by someone important, someone I love dearly. It's got my birthstone on it. I wear it all the time and it has become my good luck charm. I need it to be lucky for me today.

Today is a different day. Today is the end of the beginning, perhaps. But let me take you back, back to the day when it all started, when I was just fifteen years old. The day that changed my entire life. It was a day that started like every other. It was just an ordinary day. At least I thought it was. If I didn't go into school that day, If I had not gotten into that fight with Lucy Blackmore, then maybe things would have been different now. Maybe things would have been so very different.

I have wanted to do this for a long time, not for anyone else, but for me. Perhaps it's closure I need, and even though I have moved on with my life, I could never do this before today. There might be things in what I'm about to tell you that make you think you know where this is going. But I can assure you, you don't. So let me finish before you make any judgements. You don't know how it ends.

Are you ready? This is my story.

Chapter 1
4 Years Before...

    It was a cold Wednesday morning, which was irritating because it was meant to be summer time. I guess that's Manchester for you. I could hear the rain outside tapping on the window. I was awake but my alarm for school hadn't gone off yet. I closed my eyes hoping for another five minutes and there it was, the loud, harsh beep, constant in my ear. It was 7.30AM and the start of my day. I sat up in bed, sleep still in my eyes. My room was a small box room, but it was cosy, everything a different shade of pink. I had a bedside table next to my bed, under my window; and a clothes rail opposite. There were a few pictures that I had taken on my wall, of flowers mostly, and some bean bags and cushions on my floor. I had flower fairy lights hanging from my window and pink drape curtains behind. It was neat and tidy and it was my little hub, my safe space away from the rest of the world.

    After a few minutes of trying to wake up, I slowly got out of bed and started getting dressed for school. My school uniform was ordinary; white shirt, black skirt, tights and shoes. I always tried to make my uniform stand out, so I always wore it with a bold colour cardigan and coat. I wasn't meant to, but I used to put a little make-up on – mascara, lip-gloss, nothing too obvious. My hair was in a ponytail, tied back by a big black scrunchie. I had my own style and I wanted to express it.

I went downstairs for breakfast. The landing light was bright, there was noise coming from the TV. My little sister Chloe, ten years old, was sat on the sofa under a blanket. She was watching the same cartoon show that she watched every morning. I went into the kitchen; my mum Chrissie was stood at the kettle making me a cup of tea and my dad Jack was sat at the breakfast bar. My mum worked in retail and my dad owned his own double-glazing company. We lived in a nice, three-bed house just on the outskirts of Manchester. It had a big front drive, even bigger back garden and a huge conservatory. We had the best house on the street – I used to hear the neighbours telling my parents how nice our house was. Maggie over the road told my mum once that she always wanted to buy our house, but when it went up for sale my parents got in first. My home life and family life were really good. I was lucky.

"Morning love, here you go." Mum passed me a cup of tea. I took some fruit and walked into the living room, smiling at Dad as I passed. Chloe was still sat on the sofa. She's never been much of a morning person, so we didn't really speak. I heard Dad say goodbye to Mum, he stuck his head in to tell us to be good at school, and then he left in his car. Mum went upstairs to finish getting ready. I had my breakfast, staring at the TV without really watching it, still tired. Then I went upstairs to the bathroom, got my bag ready and headed to the door to put my shoes on. I shouted goodbye and left for school.

It was cold and wet, but not raining any more. My school was only around the corner from home, which was perfect because I was never late, unless I wanted to be. I liked school most of the time. I had a good group of friends – Lauren and Darcy were my two closest friends, we had known each other since we were babies. Our parents were all really close too. I walked in through the school gate. There were kids everywhere, teachers arriving in their cars, parents dropping kids off. It was busy, chaotic, noisy. It was just ordinary.

"Maxine!" Lauren and Darcy came running up to me. We all hugged each other. We were well liked by everyone at school, students and teachers, you could say popular. When we walked down the corridor people parted like the *Red Sea* to let us pass. Well, not really but people wanted to hang around with us. I was a good student but cheeky at times. I would push boundaries, but I was eager to learn and this shone through. Like at all schools, not everyone got on.

Lucy Blackmore was the class clown. Only thing was, she wasn't funny at all, just a pain and a distraction. She annoyed everyone. Lauren, Darcy and I spent a day in Isolation once because of her. We were messing about backstage in drama, using the props and the set to recreate scenes from famous films, Lucy came along trying to join in and ended up breaking everything. There was a show that night and Miss Conner's was not impressed. She was so angry and gave us all detention as well as a day in Isolation. It would have actually been a good day if Lucy wasn't there. No classes, just sat in a room copying a dictionary, bit boring but better than double maths and science.

Soon after we arrived at school, the bell rang and we all made our way inside. We were not in any of the same classes that day so we all went our separate ways. I had double English with Mrs Finn. I liked Mrs Finn; she was a really good teacher but if you got on the wrong side of her then you knew about it. She was a colourful character, always in floral greens and she always smelt of strong coffee. I walked into her classroom, there were a couple of other students already in there, getting their books and pens out, ready for the lesson.

"Morning Miss." I said.

"Morning Maxine." I sat down at my desk, got out my books and stared out of the window. The once busy playground was now much quieter and beautiful place to look at. I could actually see my house from the window. English was in the tower block, seven floors up so a bit of a skyscraper in our area.

It was nearly 8.20AM and the classroom started filling up. Mrs Finn started doing the register when Lucy Blackmore barged through the door laughing. Late as usual.

"Sit down." Mrs Finn was agitated. Lucy sat down in her chair, which unfortunately was on the table next to me. No effort whatsoever was ever made in terms of her appearance. Her hair always looked greasy, it was short and in a small plait. Her shirt was never done up properly and her trousers had iron marks on. She wore cheap trainers and the laces were always trailing behind. People always used to make fun of her, but she didn't seem to care, she just did her own thing. She didn't have many friends, only a few girls from the year above us who were just as bad.

Mrs Finn walked around the class handing us all a mock test. We had exams soon, so we were in full preparation mode. I wanted to do well in school. I wanted to go onto university to study fashion. To make something of myself. I was always very ambitious.

"Okay class, you have got forty-five minutes to answer the mock exam under exam conditions." Mrs Finn looked over at Lucy sternly.

"No talking, no messing about, no looking at anyone else's papers. Any questions?" The class was silent, all itching to get on with it.

"Okay, you may begin." Mrs Finn sat down at her desk and started doing some of her own paperwork.

I opened my paper and I was happy with the questions that were in front of me. I had done my revision and I felt reasonably confident. I tried to focus but I could hear Lucy sniggering. I glanced at her and gave her evils – it sounds ridiculous, but I did look at her with evil eyes. I turned back around wanting to start my paper, when a piece of paper was thrown at me. I looked up and of course it was Lucy.

"Stop it." I whispered.

"What's going on?" Mrs Finn said looking at us over her green glasses.

"Miss, I can't work with her in the classroom." I said looking at Lucy. Lucy jumped out of her seat like she had something to prove.

"Who do you think you are talking to?" she yelled. Mrs Finn stood up and came over to us in a hurry.

"That's enough! Lucy sit down please." I looked her up and down in disgust before I answered Lucy's question.

"Absolutely nothing." The class laughed; Mrs Finn took my arm to sit me down but Lucy grabbed hold of my hair. I grabbed hold of her hand on my head and with my other hand I slapped her. I actually slapped her, like maybe I fluked it but it was a proper good slap. I remember in that moment for a brief second hearing the sound it made and smiling to myself, I was proud that it wasn't a limp one. Mrs Finn tried to break us up, but the adrenaline was too much. She left the class to go and get help; the entire class was on their feet chanting my name. I didn't know what happened. I had never had a fight with anyone before. But this girl needed teaching a lesson, and no one else was going to do it. All this anger just came out of me. It was like there was no one else in the classroom, just Lucy and I.

   I managed to get her on the table and she let go of my hair. I hit her in the face again and she ripped my shirt off me. All the boys started laughing by that point because you could now see my bra. We both fell off the table and Mrs Finn came rushing in with Mrs Smith, another English teacher, and the deputy head Mr Watson. Mrs Finn put her arms around my belly from behind to prise me off Lucy, and Mrs Smith got Lucy off the floor. We were both taken out of the classroom and marched to Miss Lancashire's office. The walk seemed ages away from the classroom and the realisation of what had happened started to sink in. I felt embarrassed and disappointed in myself. Miss Lancashire was the head teacher. I had never been to her office before. I knew things were bad.

Chapter 2
The Aftermath

I was sat outside the head's office with Mrs Finn. My hair was half up, half down, my shirt ripped open and my face was bright red. It probably looked worse than it felt. Lucy was already in there probably telling loads of lies about me. But she did have a bust lip, so she ended up looking worse than me. But I knew that Lucy was no stranger to the head's office, so I was quietly confident that I would not be blamed. Mrs Finn did not say anything to me. I was expecting some kind of chat, but nothing, she almost looked disappointed that I retaliated. I smiled at her and she gave me half a smile.

The head's door opened, and Lucy came out. She had been crying. I had never seen her look vulnerable before, I almost felt sorry for her. I could hear Miss Lancashire, but couldn't see her.

"Send her home, I am expelling her for the day." Mrs Finn took Lucy and led her down the corridor. Miss Lancashire stepped into the hallway and looked at me. She did not say anything for a few seconds.

"In." I stood up and walked past her while she held the door open for me. I felt on edge. She followed me in and told me to sit down. For the first time I did not know how to react to the situation. It suddenly felt very tense. Miss Lancashire sat down and started writing something on her notebook. She was probably in her mid-thirties and very professional looking, with blonde short hair that she wore in a clip, she had glasses on, a white shirt, black blazer and black skirt with heels. She was very intimidating. I had never really spoke to her before. I had seen her around school, sometimes she spoke in assemblies, but I had never ever had a conversation with her. She started working at our school when we were in special measures. I think the school wanted a young, fresh approach to the head's position. I remember her being very popular with the staff and students when she was hired. Miss Lancashire gave no emotion, but I could still tell that she was not happy with the situation. I mean who would be. This was not ideal, especially so close to exams. I waited until she spoke to me, looking around her office discreetly.

    Her office was very clean and tidy. It smelt like lavender. There was a large desk in the middle of the room with a chair behind and two chairs in front. A small two-seater sofa under the window to the left, with a coffee table and magazines. She had filing cabinets and loads of plants around the outside. There were no pictures on the wall, just grey and white paint. It was a little empty but very neat. Minutes went past but it seemed much longer. Eventually Miss Lancashire looked up at me over her glasses.

    "Maxine, isn't it?"

    "Yes Miss."

    "I have never seen you in my office before, this is very out of character for you." I interrupted her.

    "I'm sorry Miss but she started it!"

    "You speak when I say you can speak young lady." she yelled. I had no idea why she was having a go at me like that. Like she said, this was my first time in her office and I never heard her shout at Lucy. I am sure Lucy would have answered back. I stopped talking and looked away, down to the floor.

"Now, I am going to give you after-school detention, and you can do your mock exam then." She did not look at me when she spoke, like I was just putting her out, a hassle she did not need or want. I didn't say anything else because I was scared of her reaction, although I felt it was not fair at all. She looked down at my open top.

"And for God's sake girl, go and clean yourself up." She handed me a safety pin from her desk drawer and indicated that I should leave.

I got up and left as quickly as I could, feeling uncomfortable. I gasped as the door closed behind me. Miss Lancashire's office was a place I had never been before, and I never wanted to go again. A place where every breath could be heard. It was tense and felt somewhat separate from the rest of the school. I walked to the girl's toilets where I sorted myself out and tried to wash my face without smudging my make-up. I attempted to pin my top, but it looked ridiculous and really noticeable. I left the toilets to go and get my things from Mrs Finn's class because it was still English double period. I was hoping to get some of my exam done, but when I arrived, I was asked to do something else, because my mock exam was now to be done after school.

In some ways, I felt Lucy got a better deal – at least she got to go home. I had to deal with Miss Lancashire, after-school detention and the rest of the day at school. English went past pretty quickly. I spent most of it staring into space thinking about the fight with Lucy and having to go to Miss Lancashire's office. When the bell went for break, I could not wait to get out of class, see Lauren and Darcy and fill them in on the morning I had. I put my things in my bag and headed for the door.

"Maxine, can you stay please?" I turned around and Mrs Finn waved for me to sit down. Mrs Finn spent the next fifteen minutes telling me how she expected better and I should not let Lucy get to me. Basically, the chat I wanted outside Miss Lancashire's office during class time was now taking over my entire break. Before I knew it, the bell went for third period and I had to go to science.

I made my way over to the science department. Word had clearly got around about my ordeal with Lucy and it's all people wanted to talk about. My phone was constantly buzzing from Lauren and Darcy wanting to know what was going on, much to Mr Denton's annoyance. I thought he was going to ask for my phone at one point, so I turned it off. Science was actually really good that day – we were doing experiments with jelly babies, setting them on fire. It was a nice distraction from my after-school detention.

Next class was maths with Mr Forth, which again went pretty fast because it was another mock exam, (that I managed to complete), then the bell went for dinner. I was so happy to hear that sound. I made my way to the canteen, where Lauren and Darcy were sat in our usual spot. They spotted me and jumped for me to join them. I sat down and told them everything. They were so proud of me for standing up to Lucy and wanted to know all the details. I told them about my detention after school and they also thought Miss Lancashire was being too harsh on me. I messaged my mum that afternoon to let her know and her response was not great. She already knew because Mrs Finn had called her to explain the situation. I knew she would be worried about me.

We were all in the same tutor that day, so after lunch we excitedly made our way to our tutor room. The corridors were busy with students and teachers making their way to where they needed to be. I could hear heels close by. I looked around and Miss Lancashire was walking my way, her head in loads of papers. I looked at her, but she did not notice me. She rushed past us all and down the other corridor into her office.
"You okay?" Lauren had noticed me watching her pass us.
"Yeah, fine." I replied.
We always had fun in our tutor class. Miss Adams was really nice – she was youngish, only late twenties, so we got on really well with her. She was a fun teacher, more on our level than the other older, stuffier members of staff. She had dreadlocks in her hair and she always wore it in a loose bun, with big circle glasses. All the students liked her. She treated us like adults, not kids. She worked in the art department and had a laugh with us, never taking anything too seriously. She always saw the best in a situation and when I told her what had happened that morning, she gave me some really good advice.
"You cannot change the past Maxine, only the future. So, learn from it, get through today and then back to normal tomorrow." she said with a warm smile. I really appreciated her saying that to me.
When the bell went for last period, I was usually excited because we were close to going home, but I had

the detention hanging over my head, so I was not excited at all. Although my last class that day was my favourite subject, art. I loved art, it was a module I picked along with dance, and photography. I could get creative in that class and I loved learning about different art cultures and traditions. I wasn't too bad at drawing either and I thought the subject would help me towards my fashion career goal.

    I sat down at my usual desk and Miss Lyons handed us our drawing books. She told us to choose an object in the room and sketch it. Everyone rushed up looking around trying to get their chosen items first. I looked around the room for a little while and then noticed a broken pencil on the bench. It was beautiful inside, lots of textures and designs to play around with, so I decided to think outside the box and use that for my drawing.

    Miss Lyons was a good teacher. I think she was the best dressed teacher at that school, she wore a lot of designer clothing. I would always compliment her choice of blazers. I think she was in her forties, she had long blonde hair. I had never seen anyone with such long hair before. It was always effortlessly tied back with a fancy grip. She definitely took pride in her appearance. She expected a certain behaviour from her GCSE class because we had all chosen to be there, so the setting was very professional. I felt relaxed and calm in her classes and especially on that day. Miss Lyons occasionally walked behind me, and I could feel her smile. Sometimes she took the pencil from me and sketched a little bit, so I could watch and follow. I hadn't finished my drawing when the bell went. Everyone rushed to put their things away and tidy up so they could go home. I slowly got ready for my detention.

Chapter 3
Pushing Boundaries

    The after-school detentions were always in the same room near the head's office. Lauren had been a couple of times before, for her uniform, so I knew where to go. The door was already open. James, Callum and Matt were sat scattered across the room. They were the usual type of loud, distracting kids, who came to school to just have a laugh. I got on with them, but they were shocked to see me which caused a fuss whilst I chose where to sit.

    Soon after I sat down, Mr Watson came in and told the boys to stop messing about. He handed the boys a dictionary each, the usual line-copying task. He gave me my mock exam. There was no talk from Mr Watson, just the look to begin. So I sat quietly and I did my English mock paper. It was better than I thought it would be – I felt relaxed in the quiet room without anyone to distract me. I eased into my detention and made the most of the time focusing on my paper. Before long, Mr Watson was telling us all we could leave. The boys ran out laughing and joking as if their detention was something to be proud of. I was calmer. Mr Watson came over to my desk wanting some reassurance.

    "I hope I don't see you in here again Maxine."

    "Don't worry, you won't, Sir." I left a little deflated, feeling like I had let myself down.

School was like a different place after hours. It felt daunting and the corridors seemed longer. It was quiet, almost too quiet. I found myself checking over my shoulder as I reached the door that led to the school reception area. The car park outside reception was almost empty, a few teachers just leaving or walking over to their cars. I noticed Miss Lancashire putting folders into her boot, and she noticed me as I crossed the road to exit the school gate. I smiled at her but got nothing back. I was on the path, a few minutes away from home when a car went past me and beeped. I didn't look at first, but then it beeped again. It was Miss Lancashire. I didn't see her face or anything, but I recognised the silver car from the car park. By the time I realised it was her, the car had gone. I did not know why she beeped at me when moments before she had ignored me, but Miss Lancashire could have excluded me that day, and she didn't. She did me a favour. She let me stay at school. I was grateful to her.

    That evening I sat on the sofa watching TV. Mum and Dad had a chat with me over dinner about how important school was. How I needed to keep my head down and not get distracted. I reassured them that what happened with Lucy would not happen again. They did not go on at me too much, and I was glad. They treated me maturely. I loved being at home with my little family. My parents worked hard in life and I remember from a very young age wanting to be just like them. As a family, we had everything you could ever want. We were not the richest, but we had happiness. I was such a happy child, the kid that runs to family to be picked up and cuddled, that was me. My dad was proud of us, he was proud of me. He always used to say, *"Yes our Maxine, she will be the real making of this family."* I loved hearing him say that. I was a very lucky girl. I was exhausted that night, but I could not get to sleep. I was tossing and turning looking at the flower shapes my fairy lights were making on my walls. I barely closed my eyes and soon enough it was 7.30AM again and the start of another day.

    My school routine was always pretty much the same, so I won't bore you with repeating everything. A few days later I was in maths. I was asked to go and pick up some work sheets from the staff room that Mr Fourth had forgot. I didn't mind at all; it was only at the other side of the building. I passed the toilet block to make sure I looked okay. I always did that at any opportunity. I always wanted to look good. I made my way down to the staff room and knocked on the door. There was no answer, so I just walked in. I had not been in the staff room before. It looked secretive. I remember thinking if those walls could talk, the stories they could tell. There were lots of blue sofas around, coffee tables, coffee machines, a kitchen area and an admin area. It was neat and tidy and smelled of coffee. I'd learned that teachers need a lot of coffee to get through the day.
    I made my way over to the printer which is where Mr Fourth had told me he left the papers we needed. I found them straight away. Miss Lancashire walked in not long after me and went to the coffee machine. She didn't notice me at first and then she turned in my direction.
    "What are you doing in here?"
    "Just picking up some papers for Mr Fourth."

"Hurry up please." She turned back around and I walked out.
"Bye Maxine." I heard from behind. I looked back at her; she was fiddling with the coffee machine. I smiled to be polite, but I did not say anything. Miss Lancashire made me feel on edge, she had this presence about her. I never knew how to take her. But Miss Lancashire did end up excluding Lucy for the rest of that week, so I felt I could relax for a bit in classes. I was hoping she would not come back. The school was a much better place without her. We got so much more work done.

In photography, I got a nice surprise when Lauren ended up joining our class. She had mentioned to her media studies teacher that she wanted to use one of our cameras to help her with her exam piece, so she had been sent over to work on her project. Lauren was so talented – she wanted to be a TV presenter, she had a plan to go onto college to study TV and film for a few years and then apply for placements. She loved being in front of the camera, she had a YouTube channel and always got positive feedback. Darcy wanted to work with young children or animals, she could never decide. And of course, I loved all things fashion, so we were a creative bunch. Lauren was sat on a computer away from us all, we didn't chat much but it was nice to have her there.

For my photography exam I had decided to take pictures of my family and friends faces. I also took some celebrity pictures off the internet too. I cut them all up and then merged them all together to create one new face. Through photography, I was tackling the theme of gender, race, religion and age in an abstract way. The idea that we are all living as one. I still have that work somewhere. I used a black canvas as the frame which made it look very professional, like something you would see in a shop. I was so impressed with how that piece turned out. My teacher Miss Jade said that it was one of the best pieces of work that we as a class had submitted. I was chuffed with the feedback.

    It was a double photography session and I remember my eyes going funny. I had spent hours cutting up pictures and carefully sticking them together. I looked over to Lauren who was stretching and seemed to be wanting a break too. She leaned back in her chair and looked in my direction. She whispered for me to follow her. Lauren went to Miss Jade and told her she needed to go back to her class to get some feedback on what she was working on. She left and a few minutes later I asked if I could go to the toilet.

    I met Lauren outside class and we headed outside. It was nice to be in the fresh air, it was very stuffy in the classroom we were working in. We walked to the school field and sat on a bench behind one of the basketball courts. We did not make a habit of skipping lessons, lying to teachers, sneaking off. But we had done so much work that day, school life was coming to an end so we decided we could take five minutes out. It was not five minutes; we were sat on that bench for nearly forty minutes. When we realised how long we had been, we both panicked, nervously laughing as we tried to work out what to say.

    We crept from the back of the field into the building trying to avoid seeing any teachers. We had only just got back into the photography department when we saw Miss Jade walking towards us.

"I expect better of you two." Miss Jade looked disappointed. We had nothing to say, nothing that would get us out of trouble so we both just said sorry. Miss Jade led the way back to class, shaking her head in frustration. We followed with a sigh of relief that she was not yelling at us.

When I think about school, I am glad I had those mischievous moments, how boring and dull would it have been if we had just played by all the rules. We did not even make it back to class when the bell went. We got our bags to head for lunch, but Miss Jade told us to sit down, she had not finished with us yet.

We sat in silence next to each other whilst Miss Jade sat on her desk watching our every move. Ten minutes later Miss Lancashire walked in. I hid my head in my hands and could not believe that yet again I was finding myself in trouble. I was so scared of Miss Lancashire yelling at me.

"Right, what's happened? Maxine again." Miss Lancashire got herself a chair, shaking her head disapprovingly. She looked at me first and then over to Lauren, she sat in front of us waiting for us to respond.

"Sorry Miss, we just went for some fresh air." Lauren looked at me for support.

"If you wanted some air, you could have gone for a few minutes, not over half an hour! I do not like been lied to." Miss Jade was irritated with us both.

"Sorry Miss, it won't happen again." I said, genuinely feeling guilty about the situation. Miss Lancashire sat back in her chair, folding her arms.

"I have not had to deal with either of you before, and now with you Maxine, it's getting to be every other day."

"Sorry Miss Lancashire." I said.

"Right, go and get your lunch, both of you and then you're going to come back here and make up the time you have lost."

I sighed, looking over to Lauren.

"You have something to say Maxine?" I shook my head, trying to avoid eye contact with her.

"Off you go." Miss Lancashire watched as Lauren and I left the classroom.

Chapter 4
Round Two

    I adored Fridays, I loved the lessons – double art first, and then I had a PE class with Lauren and Darcy which was usually good fun. I quickly got settled in class. It was quieter than usual because some of the other students were working on their exam projects in another classroom. I remember looking around almost sighing with contentment. I was lost in my own world in those classes. Miss Lyons used to put classical music on to help relax us. It was very atmospheric and really helped us stay focused on our projects. I was still working on my pencil drawing and I had started applying colour. Miss Lyons was very impressed with my idea and where I wanted to take it. I was planning to make the sketch 3D using fabrics textures and making it more of a sensory art piece with smell sections. Ambitious I know, but I enjoyed the challenge and Miss Lyons said that there had never been anything done like that before. She said if I could pull it off in a stylised way then I could be certain of top marks.

    Our art class looked out onto the car park, it had big windows, so we could see the front field. After a while I was distracted by some movement outside. I looked out and saw Miss Lancashire with another student, it looked intense, like she was telling him off. I felt sorry for him. I knew how it felt to be on the wrong side of her. I watched for a while until the student walked away in a huff.

"Dan, do not walk away from me." I heard Miss Lancashire shout through the open window. I hadn't seen Dan around school before. I think he was in the year below. He didn't stop and carried on walking further away from her, I didn't blame him. Miss Lancashire paced for a little while, said something into her walkie talkie that she carried around and then looked in my direction. I turned away and got on with my work. About half an hour later Miss Lancashire walked into our art class and went to talk to Miss Lyons. I couldn't help but look. Miss Lancashire looked at me moments later and pointed at me to follow her out the room. I didn't want to go anywhere with her, but I had no choice. I followed her outside the classroom, where she stopped and turned around to me in the corridor.

"Will you come to my office at lunch?"
I nodded politely.

"Good. Go back to class Maxine." Miss Lancashire noticed Mr Watson down the corridor and hurried to meet him. I watched until she was out of sight and then I went back to class and got on with my work. The bell soon rang and it was lunch time. I had knots in my stomach as I took the walk to Miss Lancashire's office. I knocked on her door, apprehensive to what was going to be said, to how she was going to be with me. I didn't know why I was there.

"Come in." Miss Lancashire was sat at her desk typing on her computer. She did not look at me but ushered me to sit down. When she looked up, she seemed more welcoming than she had been before.

"How was your detention the other day?"
"It was okay, I managed to finish my paper."

"Yes, I was talking to Mrs Finn, she said you did very well." Miss Lancashire handed me an exam paper from her drawer. It was my English mock grade. I got an A. I could not believe it. I was so happy with myself. I knew I could do it.

"Well done Maxine." Miss Lancashire smiled for the first time, sitting back in her chair more relaxed.

"Thank you." I looked intensely at my paper, not knowing what else to say. I could feel Miss Lancashire staring at me.

"Go and get some lunch." Miss Lancashire sat up in her chair and continued doing her work, typing heavily at her computer. I quietly left.

Monday morning: the hardest day of the week for everyone. I woke up ready for the day ahead. Finally, the weather had started to pick up and the sun was beaming through my bedroom window. I had forgotten that this was the day Lucy was back from being excluded.

In English, Mrs Finn was looking over some different exam questions with us. Suddenly the door bursts open and in walked Lucy. Everyone sighed, and I put my head in my hands. She sat down, and Mrs Finn went over to her.

"Please behave yourself."

"Chance would be a fine thing." I muttered quietly, or so I thought, but Lucy heard me which really wound her up. It was like round one all over again, although this time it was me egging her on. Mrs Finn looked at me in disbelief but I carried on. I didn't know why. It was like word vomit.

All the years of frustration I had towards Lucy came out in a split second. I commented on Lucy's hair, her trainers, her clothes and I kept going on and on until she snapped and then went for me. Mrs Finn stood in the middle of us and managed to calm the situation, but she asked me to stay behind at break. She had the chat with me like she had before. I had no answer for her as to why I acted like I did. I apologised and headed to break, but I could tell by the way Mrs Finn walked away from me that she was concerned.

"You know Maxine, I expect better of you." she said. I was starting to hear that saying a lot.

I went into the canteen to meet Lauren and Darcy. I told them that Lucy was back but they already knew. We were chatting about this and that when Lucy threw a yoghurt at me, out of nowhere. She just walked up to the food counter, grabbed a yoghurt and threw it. It went all down my top and in my hair. I was done with her. I got up from my seat and ran at her. She gave as good back and yet again we were scrapping, like animals in a zoo, being watched by all the other students, dinner ladies and some supply teachers that were too scared to get involved. A loud whistle was blown, and Miss Lancashire and Mr Watson rushed in to part us. Miss Lancashire took hold of me.

"Stop it now! Maxine, get off her!" she yelled. She was really strong and literally carried me to her office. Mr Watson was walking with Lucy behind. He took her to his office for a telling off. I think they wanted to keep us separate. Students were laughing and pointing, this was their entertainment, but it was just embarrassing. Miss Lancashire threw me into her office.

"What on earth are you playing at Maxine? Is this the new you? Someone who makes trouble, causes fights, hurts people? Look at me when I am talking to you."

"She threw a yoghurt at me." My voice was small and my eyes started to water. The realisation of where I was again made me feel sick. I had no idea why all of a sudden Lucy was getting to me more than usual, why all of a sudden I felt out of control. I looked up to Miss Lancashire, her face was red from all the yelling. Her office door opened.

"Miss Lancashire." Mr Watson walked in.

"I have called Lucy's Mum, she is coming to get her, shall I ring Maxine's?" There was a pause. Miss Lancashire stood, hands on hips, looking at me. I couldn't hold back the tears that were pooling in my eyes, they started to spill silently down my cheeks.

"No, she is going to Isolation for the rest of the week." Mr Watson looked a little puzzled, nodded and left. I stood; my face wet from all the crying. Miss Lancashire moved closer to me.

"Crying will not work with me young lady. Now go and clean yourself up." She said sternly, opening her office door for me to leave. I headed to the toilets and locked myself in a cubicle. I sat on the toilet seat, still covered in yoghurt, tired and fed up. I wanted to go home, I would have rather been excluded too.

After about half an hour I got the courage to leave the toilet block and headed to Isolation. I managed to get some of the yoghurt off, but my top was stained and smelt horrible. I was the only one in Isolation, with one of the supply teachers who were shocked to see me. But I was glad that I was the only student. I did not want anyone seeing me look such a mess.

    In Isolation you're just sat in a room, in silence with no motivation, stimulation, nothing. I sat down at the desk where there was a notebook, a pencil and a dictionary. I opened the book and started copying it page by page. I was so bored. Hours passed very slowly. I was about five pages into copying the dictionary when Miss Lancashire walked in with my stuff. I had completely forgotten about my bag and coat that I had left in the canteen.
    "I'll take over now." Miss Lancashire sat down and started writing some things down in her notebook. I wanted to say something to the supply teacher, tell her not to leave, but I was exhausted and did not want to get into any more trouble. I looked down to the dictionary, but I could feel Miss Lancashire watching me. After a few minutes I looked up at her.
    "Do I scare you?" she asked. I didn't say anything. I thought it was a strange thing to ask me. Miss Lancashire walked over to my desk and leaned on it in front of me.
    "Do I scare you?" she repeated. I still did not answer the question.
    "Miss, please can I go home?"
    "You're not going anywhere Maxine. I will be keeping my eye on you from now on."
Miss Lancashire sat back down. Not long after the bell went to go home.
    "I'll take you home."
    "No, I'm okay."
    "I was not asking Maxine. Get your stuff. Move it."

I remember getting into her car and not being able to look at her. She dropped me off just at the end of my road.

"Now for the rest of the week you are going to do your time in Isolation, and then I never want to see you in the state you have been in recently, do you understand?" I nodded.

"I can't hear you Maxine."

"Yes Miss."

"I would hate to have to come to your house and speak to your parents in person." She looked over the road, as though she already knew which house was mine. I got out of the car and walked home.

When I walked through the door, the house was busy because it was teatime. Mum and Dad wanted a chat about the events which led to one week in Isolation, but I just walked upstairs and got into bed. I said I did not feel well, and they did not bother me again about it for the rest of the night. I laid in bed, overthinking everything. I could not get Miss Lancashire out of my head. Mum brought me up some tea and toast, but I was not hungry.

When I got up the next day, my parents were looking suspicious. They were sat in the kitchen at the breakfast bar. They clearly had something on their mind, Mum handed me a letter. I leaned on the breakfast bar, already worn out by the week.

"Read it." Mum said.

"What is it?"

"Just read it." she repeated.

Dear Mr and Mrs Watts,

I hope you are well.
I am writing to you regarding Maxine's recent behaviour. She is now a cause for concern. It is very out of character for her which is why the decision has been taken to punish her so firmly, especially since she is so close to her exams. The behaviour she has been displaying recently is not something we as a school tolerate, especially with a student who usually shows so much potential. I really want to nip this in the bud and get Maxine back on track. I have put Maxine in Isolation for the rest of week, she can use the time to study for her exams. This is something I will allow. I will be keeping an eye on her and monitoring her progress.

If you want to make any further enquiries or ask any questions, please do not hesitate to contact me.

Kindest of regards,
Jane Lancashire, B.E.D

Mum and Dad waited for me to respond.
    "I guess I am just stressed out with my exams coming up. I will do well, I promise." Mum and Dad told me that I just had to focus on the next few months and then I would be able to relax. They said that they were proud of me and it would all be worth it in the end. I appreciated them not yelling at me, they treated me like an adult. I loved my parents. I wanted to make them so proud. I don't think I have, but I always intended to.

Chapter 5
Isolation

My week in Isolation went very slowly. I was joined by some of the most disruptive students in my year, all trying to play up and show off. I did not belong there. Supply teacher after supply teacher came to sit with us like we were babies. My GCSEs were coming up and I was losing time. I needed to prepare in class with my teachers. It was frustrating. The only good thing about being in Isolation was the peace and quiet, most of the time. It was so quiet you could hear a pin drop.

There was not many of us in Isolation that week, a few students that I had seen around school but I had no idea who they were. Matt was in there too, but he was doing less time than me. He got a few days for leaving class and back chatting a teacher. Sounds like a prison sentence, doesn't it? What are you in for? How much time did you get? I was happy to see him, having a familiar face made it more bearable.

When you're in Isolation you have to eat dinner in silence too. You could bring a packed lunch that you had to eat in a separate room, or you were escorted by staff to the canteen to pick up your food and then taken back to the room. A staff member would sit with you until you were back in Isolation copying the dictionary. You could go the whole school day without saying a single word. I had a full week of that to look forward to. Miss Lancashire did keep her promise and allowed me to use the time to study for my exams. I went at the beginning of each day to my module teachers and got given work that I should have been doing in class. So after a while it felt like being sat in a library. I started that week feeling very productive. I tried to make the best out of a bad situation and study for my exams.

However, I soon got frustrated because there were some questions that I had been set that I did not understand. I needed my teachers to help me through parts, to give me feedback and tell me what to work on. My exams were less than one month away and having that week out of my usual routine, usual class was starting to take it's toll. I knew I was better than that. On the Wednesday morning I sat quietly, looking around at the other students who were getting on with their task. I was getting the courage to ask the supply teacher who was watching us if I could go back to class. I must have sat there for a good twenty minutes working out how to go about the situation, playing out different scenarios in my head. Eventually I got the courage to put my hand up. The supply teacher spotted me and waved at me to go outside with him.

I think the supply teacher was called Mr Benson – he was tall, skinny, with long brown hair and very little patience.

"What is it?"

"Sir, please can I go back to class?"

"No."

"Why?" I snapped.

"Maxine, I am not starting a conversation with you about this. You don't get to choose how long you're in

Isolation for." I did give him some attitude because I did not like him at all. Mr Benson saw another teacher walking down the corridor and he asked if she would watch over Isolation for a few minutes whilst he dealt with me.

"Sir, please?"
"Right Maxine, come with me."
"Where are we going?"
"To see Miss Lancashire."
"What? No. I only wanted to go back to my class. I don't want to make it worse." He did not say anything as he marched in front of me to Miss Lancashire's office. I was panicking like I had never panicked before. All I could think about was how angry she was going to be when she saw me again. How she was going to shout at me. I kept thinking, *oh my God she is actually going to kill me.*

Mr Benson knocked on Miss Lancashire's office door. I hoped she would not be in. I didn't want to see her. But soon enough her voice could be heard telling us to go in. I followed Mr Benson into her office. Miss Lancashire was sat at her desk, surrounded by paperwork like usual.

"I have got Maxine Watts with me." I stood in the doorway awkwardly, trying to hide behind Mr Benson. Miss Lancashire looked at me over her glasses.

"Thank you Mr Benson, I'll deal with her."
Mr Benson left.

"Again Maxine? This better be good." She was not as snappy with me as I thought she would be. I walked a little closer to her desk.

"I just asked if I could go back to class. I'm wasting my time in there on my own."

"You are not going back to class until next week, let this be a lesson to you." I sighed and felt agitated.

"You only have two days left." I nodded and gave up the fight. Miss Lancashire walked me back to Isolation.

"You have been doing your exam prep haven't you?"

"Yes Miss."

"Then this is not a waste of time." She opened the door for me. I sat back down. Miss Lancashire looked over to Mr Benson.

"Make sure she does not wander off." I looked down at my papers and tried to make plan. I just had to deal with it.

After school I decided to go to my art class. Miss Lyons was sat at her computer at the front of the class, she noticed me walking over to her.

"Everything okay Maxine?"

"Please can I stay behind to do some work? I'm sick of being in Isolation."

"Yes Maxine, course you can, I have to rush off this evening, but you can stay for an hour or so." I smiled, a little deflated.

I got myself set up at my usual desk. It felt amazing to be back in the classroom working on my project properly, not closed up in a little room like a prisoner. I was so content in the quiet that I did not even notice Miss Lyons leave. I sat staring out of the window for a while, it was very peaceful and calm. All of a sudden, I heard some noise close to the classroom and I noticed Miss Lancashire stood in the corridor speaking with another teacher. I didn't want her to notice me. It was like she was following me, everywhere I was she also seemed to be. I thought about closing the classroom door but it was too late, her eyes made contact with mine. I turned away from her and I started shading my drawing. Not long after I heard the door close behind me. I looked around and Miss Lancashire was stood staring at me. I didn't say anything and carried on drawing.

    Miss Lancashire walked over to me, she stood behind me putting her hands on my shoulders. I stopped drawing and just stared ahead, not moving.

    "That's beautiful. Is that what you want to be, an artist?"

    "I want to work in fashion, if I'm good enough."

    "Isn't that something that someone else tells you? If you are good enough? All you can do is work hard and try. And I see no reason why you couldn't be good enough." Miss Lancashire said leaning over me and touching my drawing with one of her hands.

    "I suppose so."

    "You have a real gift Maxine." Miss Lancashire moved from behind me and sat on the chair next to me. She moved closer towards me, moving my hair behind my ear. I couldn't look at her at first, but slowly my eyes met hers. She had such an intimidating presence, every time I found myself with her she made me feel nervous. I could feel my body start to shake.

    "A real gift." she repeated. I smiled slightly. After a few moments Miss Lancashire stood up.

    "You should go home soon, get some rest." I watched her leave the classroom in a blur.

    That night I sat in my room and I could not stop thinking about what happened in art with Miss Lancashire. Nothing happened but it felt different to how it felt before. I did not say anything to Mum and Dad, but I drafted a message to send to Lauren and Darcy.

Maxine
So something happened today, it was a little bit strange. I stayed behind in art to do some work and Miss Lancashire came into the classroom, closed the door and stood behind me. She started talking to me about what I wanted to do, she was actually being nice, but I felt intimidated.

And then I read it back and realised how stupid it sounded, so I deleted the message and did not say anything. I thought about Miss Lancashire until I fell asleep. I could not think about anyone else.

Chapter 6
The Head

    On the Friday, just after dinner, the bell rang. It was assembly time and even though we were in Isolation we had to go to assembly. It was always held in the drama hall, which had big black curtains around the outside. They would always be closed which made the space more intimate. Rows of brown chairs were placed in the middle of the hall, and teachers would stand around the side. We had to sit in our Isolation group higher up at the back. It was awkward, all the other students looked at us as we sat in our seats, some pointed and laughed when they saw me. I was so embarrassed.
    The usual stuff was talked about in assemblies, by lots of different teachers. What was happening in and around the school, improvements staff were working on, extra modules being offered to us. Usually I found all this interesting, but I just wanted to leave. I felt judged. One of the teachers were finishing up when Miss Lancashire appeared from behind the curtain. She took over and gave us a massive speech on how important the next few months were leading up to our exams. She glanced over the students until she spotted me. I looked down at the floor, avoiding any eye contact. Everything she talked about I felt was about me. Maybe I was being paranoid. But she told a story of how she had known a student who was the perfect student. Until just before her exams when

she got with the wrong crowd and ultimately failed everything.

"Please do well, please do your best, please be the best you can be." Miss Lancashire finished. I looked up and she was still looking at me. I turned away again, everyone was being directed and co-ordinated out by the teachers. Our small Isolation group was led back too. Before we left the hall I looked over my shoulder, Miss Lancashire had gone. I don't know why but I wished when I turned around, she was still stood there. Maybe I wanted to say thank you to her, she had cut me a lot of slack. I didn't know why she kept me in school, but I assume she must had believed in me.

Over the weekend, Dad was working overtime, so it was just me, Mum and Chloe. We all went for an afternoon tea at our favourite place called *Monroe's* in central Manchester. It was a vintage feature place with low lighting and classical music. Everything was deep red and browns and very atmospheric. Instead of hardback chairs, the seating was lounge sofas and chairs, very comfy and so soft. It was like a home away from home. It was very relaxing and the afternoon tea itself was delicious. The perfect place to go after everything that seemed to be going on at school.

"You alright love?" Mum sounded worried.

"Yeah, I've just had a rubbish week." I replied. Mum took hold of my hand.

"You are a good girl Maxine. I am so proud of you. You got in a situation with this girl but you have not lost anything, you can still get those grades. Put last week behind you." I gave her a hug, thanking her.

"I want a new backpack for tonight." Chloe interrupted us, she was going to her first sleepover that night, so it's all she wanted to talk about. Her friend Beth only lived over the road but she felt so grown up. It was great spending some girly time with Mum and Chloe, especially after my week in Isolation. I was excited to get back to school and to be back in the classroom. But I did have something on my mind, something I wanted to talk about, but I couldn't, not to anyone.

During mid-week tutor, Miss Adams told me that Miss Lancashire wanted to see me in her office. I had that feeling in my stomach that I got every time I had to go and see her. A nervous feeling, because I never knew what to expect with her. I knocked on her office door and I heard Miss Lancashire tell me to go in.

"Sit down Maxine, do you want some tea?" I was a little confused, but I decided to be polite.

"Sure, thank you." Miss Lancashire left to make the tea. I sat quietly looking around, wondering why I was there. After a few minutes Miss Lancashire walked in with a tray. She placed it on her desk and gave me a cup. She made the tea for us both.

"How are you getting on after the last few weeks?"

"I'm doing alright. I don't know what got into me." I took a sip of my tea which was too hot to drink.

"Well that's good to hear, it would be such a shame for you to mess up all your exams now, you have clearly worked hard during your school life." The bell went for last period. Neither of us moved.

"Shall I go to class now?"

"You should." Miss Lancashire walked to the door and opened it. I followed her to the door and was about to walk out when she closed it.

"What do you want to do Maxine?"

"What do you mean?"

"You can stay and help me if you want?" The feeling in the room changed. It felt like the staff room felt when I picked up those maths papers, it felt secretive. Even though she did scare me and made me feel uneasy, I did want to stay.

"Okay." Miss Lancashire smiled at me softly and gestured at me to sit back down. She leant over me, picking up her phone on her desk.

"Hello, this is Miss Lancashire, could you let Maxine Watts teacher know she will not be coming into class? She is helping me with some exam prep, thank you." She put the phone down and went back behind her desk, rustled through her drawer for a few seconds and put a large folder on her desk.

"This was last year's exam questions and answers."

"Should you be showing me these?"

"I'm not showing you anything Maxine." Miss Lancashire passed me the folder. I looked at her unsure about what to do. I eventually took the folder and held it.

"Would you do this for anyone else?" I asked, still confused.

Miss Lancashire turned to her computer, ignoring my question, she started typing. I could not help but smile. Miss Lancashire had been there these past few weeks when I was a bit of a mess. I suppose she wanted to make sure I was on the right path. I took out a pen and paper and started making detailed notes. I stayed with her all afternoon until it was home time.

"Thank you." I handed Miss Lancashire the folder back.

"Keep up the good work Maxine. Probably best not to tell anyone about the tea and missing class. I don't want to be swamped with students all wanting my time and attention like this."

"I won't Miss."

"Oh, and the exam papers I have shown you, that goes no further."

"What exam paper?" I said with a little confidence. Miss Lancashire laughed. I got my things together and left her office.

"Bye Miss." I smiled at her with the door closing behind me.

Over the past month leading up to my exams, I was heavily involved in my studies. I barely saw friends and family because I was making final adjustments to my work and getting everything together. I was finishing my photography and art projects ready to be marked during break and lunch time. I had worked on my portfolios for those subjects whilst at home, so I was very pleased with the amount and quality of work I was submitting. I was preparing to dance my solo and group dance for my moderator and getting ready to sit my English, maths and science exams.

Finally, the time had come to put all the years of work into practice and gain something to show for it. I was so determined to get the grades that I had been predicted. Any bit of free time I had went into my studies. I became very overwhelmed and emotional. Things really got on top of me one day after school and I ended up running into the toilets and just sobbing. This was the time of my life that would determine what happened next. There was a lot riding on it. The toilet block was near Miss Lancashire's office and after about twenty minutes, I decided to go and see her. I don't know why but she was the first person to come to mind. I knocked on her door but there was no answer. I thought she had gone home but not long after she walked past me sat on a bench near her office. She noticed me straight away.

"Hey, what's up with you?"

"It's nothing Miss." I said wiping my eyes with my sleeve.

"Well, it's clearly something." Miss Lancashire put her hands on her hips. She knelt down in front of me.

"Maxine, can you handle half a cider?" I looked up at her wiping my eyes, wondering if she was being serious. She looked like she was, and I was too shocked to react.

"Come on." We walked to her office and then to her car, she told me to text my mum and to let her know I was staying behind at school, which I did. The car park was very quiet at that time. No one in sight. A cleaner did pass us and Miss Lancashire acknowledged her. I did not react.

Miss Lancashire drove us to a country pub *The Black Swan* about twenty five minutes outside of Manchester. She bought me half a cider, she had red wine. We sat in one of the booths, it was not very busy and even though I did feel a little bit awkward at first being outside of school with the head teacher, no one knew us and no one was staring.

"Don't be nervous Maxine." I took a sip of my drink and eased into my chair.

"I really want to do well in my exams Miss."

"You have prepared, haven't you?"

"Yeah."

"Then next week, you sit your exams and do your best, that's all you can do. I have seen the work you are submitting and it's very good. The practical dance exam you have danced many times before, and the sit-down ones? You just take it question by question, take your time and stay focused."

"Why are you doing this for me?"

"You have a lot of potential Maxine."

"I am sorry for how I behaved Miss." Miss Lancashire touched my hand with hers. For the first time in that moment, I felt like she cared for me. She cared about me doing well and about my future.

"I know you are. Right Maxine, can you handle another?" I laughed. She bought us another drink and then took me home.
I couldn't believe I was thinking it, but I liked her. I really liked her.

Chapter 7
Exams

The Saturday before we started taking our exams, Lauren and Darcy came over to mine for a sleepover. We had sleepovers a lot, we always took it in turns. They came around at 6.30PM. Mum always made a massive effort with sleepovers, she made us a buffet to eat and decorated the dining room in banners and balloons. It looked like it could have been someone's birthday. Chloe loved it when Lauren and Darcy came around, she loved hanging out with them, she felt really grown up. We danced to music, did our hair, gave Chloe a makeover and then the best part, getting snuggled in our PJ's.

We settled in my room to watch a film. Chloe fell asleep halfway through so Mum took her to bed. After the film we made hot chocolates and snuggled back in my room, the floor full of large fluffy cushions, pillows and bean bags.

"I can't wait to take my exams. I just need a break." I said.

"Was your week in Isolation not enough?" Darcy said laughing. I threw a cushion at her.

"It was funny though!" she insisted.

"So, what actually happened the other day?" Lauren asked, sipping her drink.

"What do you mean?"

"The other day in tutor when you had to go see Miss Lancashire, you never came back?" I took a sip of my hot chocolate whilst thinking about my answer.

"Maxine!" They both shouted, annoyed by my hesitation.

"She just wanted to know how I was getting on, she made us some tea, and..." I was interrupted by Lauren.

"What? That's weird."

"Why?" I said, feeling defensive of the situation.

"She's the head teacher, it's just weird." After I heard their reaction and had seen the look on their faces, I decided not to tell them about missing class. And definitely not about her taking me for some drinks.

"She was just being nice, not weird." Lauren and Darcy looked at each other.

"So how do you feel about your exams?" I asked, aiming to sway the conversation. We chatted for a while, mostly about the new PE teacher- Mr Dyer. Lauren and Darcy were obsessed with him. He was fresh out of university, blond hair, blue eyes, tanned skin- very cute.

"I cannot wait for PE next week." Lauren said with a huge grin on her face.

"Sir! Sir! I think I have pulled a muscle." she continued, stroking her leg.

"He is so fit though, isn't he?" Darcy said aiming the question at me.

"Yeah, really fit." I said trying to join in. When Lauren and Darcy eventually fell asleep, I kept thinking about their reaction to what I had told them. Boundaries had been crossed- yes, but nothing inappropriate had actually happened. I was so sure it hadn't.

When I came to sit my exams, I was so nervous. I remember sitting my first one which was English Literature. We used to do our exams in the big gym hall in the PE department. It was one of those big, cold, echoey places where every sound was enhanced. There were rows and rows of tables and chairs, there must have been nearly one hundred small tables. I was sat on the left-hand side. All the students including myself were scanning the room trying to spot our friends. Staff were coming and going, teachers from all around the school popping in and out. There were exam moderators at the front preparing our exam papers ready to be handed out. It all seemed very hectic.

The hall started filling up quickly with students. I looked to see Lauren and Darcy and waved to them as they headed for the back of the hall. They waved back, then a staff member stood in between them and looked at me to turn around. They were always very strict when it came to exams. No talking, looking around at people, you couldn't even breathe loudly. It was a very tense atmosphere and it did not help that all the students were very nervous and apprehensive too.

Two large clocks hung from the front walls, one to the left and one to the right, a constant reminder of how much time we had on each exam question. They did not make any noise; the handles would just slowly move round and round and round. It started getting quieter with just the slight bustle of teachers chatting, no specific conversation could be heard, it just sounded like one big mumble.

Miss Lancashire walked into the hall with a clipboard, you could hear her heels from down the corridor. She went straight to the front of the hall and started talking to one of the moderators. The students all sat quietly as one of the exam moderators had begun to give the exam papers out, placing one white booklet on each desk. Each student watched, waiting in anticipation for theirs to arrive. I just stared at Miss Lancashire. She had such an aura, controlling the entire room. She gave her clipboard to the exam moderator she was talking to and headed out. I watched her leave, and hoped that she would notice me. On her way out, she passed my desk and looked down at me.

"Good luck Maxine." I smiled as she left and waited for my exam paper to begin.

Chapter 8
School's Out

The last day of school soon came around. It was a strange feeling knowing I would never put my school uniform on again. I was excited about my last day – exams were over and activities were being organised for us. We also had a special achievement assembly to look forward to, where students would be given certificates and other treats from our teachers. Miss Lancashire was going to be finishing the day with a special speech. So it was an exciting school day and one that I did not want to miss.

When we arrived at school that day, some students were in their own clothing. I suppose they thought they would get away with whatever they wanted since it was the last day. Some of them were probably not going back anyway so boundaries were pushed. For me, the last day of school was not about testing the teachers patience, it was about appreciating every moment before it was over. Lucy did not even bother to show up, not that I was particularly surprised.

There was nothing to do in our classes, so we spent the time signing our shirts and our books. We were also allowed to look through our past work and take it home if we wanted to. It was such a nice, relaxed atmosphere. Everyone was in such a good mood, students and teachers. I had brought one of my own books from home for people to sign. Mum had bought it for me. It was silver and black, with the word *Memories* written on the front. Each page was dedicated to one person. I gave it to every person I came into contact with. Everyone wrote such nice things to me, wishing me well, telling me how amazing I was, how they knew I was going to go on to do great things. It was very overwhelming. I loved signing other people's too. I thought it was such a nice idea for us all, to one day be able to look back on.

I wasn't sure if I wanted to get my T-shirt signed at first but I soon got carried away in the moment. We used black marker to destroy our once-white shirts, in the best possible way of course. The teachers had a laugh with us too. Mrs Finn even had a laugh with me about my recent behaviour. It was light-hearted and all in good fun but basically, she said that she was worried about me for a while and it was nice to see me back to normal. I found myself talking to students who I had never spoken to before, the book signing really brought the year group together. It was nice to talk to people who usually you would just pass in the corridor.

After tutor we had a two hour assembly to look forward too. Miss Adams took our tutor group into the assembly hall, which was decorated with balloons and *Good Luck* banners. The song *We Are The Champions* was playing in the background as we all walked in. All the chairs were set up like usual, and at the front there was a reading desk for the teachers to go and stand behind to talk to us. There was also a table full of certificates and other prizes on it. It all looked a bit chaotic with so much going on. It felt very different to usual assemblies, there was a different kind of energy. Everyone seemed positive and in a care free mood.

Once everyone was seated, students and teachers waited, aiming their attention to the front of the hall. The music gradually got quieter and the mumbling of students and teachers could be heard. Miss Lancashire walked in from the back of the hall to the front and stood behind the stand, she turned to look at us all.

"Good afternoon everyone. I must say how lovely you all look in your new uniform." she said looking at us over her glasses. We all laughed. Miss Lancashire continued.

"I have been a head teacher at this school for nearly three years now and the potential going forward in this room is the highest of any year group. I know you are going to go on to do amazing things, but I want to take you back to when it all started." Miss Lancashire moved to one side, and a projector that was hanging at the back started to come on. The lights went off and a video started. It was a ten minute video made of clips and photos of all of us; trips we had been on with school, drama productions, charity days, non-uniform days. Inspirational quotes popped up throughout along with clips of the teachers wishing us well, all to sad music. This set the room off in floods of tears. Lauren and Darcy started crying which set me off. We all must have looked a right state because when the lights went back on Mr Benton looked at us all and shouted,

"Bloody hell, turn them back off!"

The entire assembly laughed. Once everyone had calmed down, Miss Lancashire stood behind the stand again.

"I know you have all got your own hopes and dreams, different goals in life, and whether you have enjoyed school life or hated it, there is not a single teacher in this room that is not behind you, wishing you the very best, myself included. So go from here today, go and get your dreams, go and achieve, but go and do it the right way like we in this room have spent years drilling into you." Miss Lancashire smiled at us and we all applauded.

It was time for the awards. They were silly, for things like- *bad hair, most annoying, cheekiest, most hard-working.* Just light-hearted fun, all voted for by our year group. Lauren got *prettiest* which of course, she deserved, although I should have totally got it (only joking). Darcy got *clumsiest* which was funny because she almost fell over her bag when she walked to the front. I got *most determined* which I was chuffed about. Every student got one award which consisted of a certificate and plastic trophy.
"I would actually like to throw my own in." Miss Lancashire reached for another trophy.
"This is for the *wild child,* come on Maxine." I was so embarrassed and put my head in my hands. Everyone was laughing and clapping as I walked to the front.
"Thanks Miss." I said, red in the face. Miss Lancashire along with everyone else was laughing. I could not wait to sit back in my seat.
The rest of the assembly was spent mingling with everyone, saying our goodbyes. I drifted from Lauren and Darcy to talk to my teachers, and to tell them what my plans were. I found myself in a crowd of students, all chatting about what we're doing over summer. Miss Lancashire made her way over to us. She was making sure she spoke to everyone.

"What's your plan then Maxine?"

"I want to come back next year to do my A-levels."

"You're coming back then, I will look forward to it!" Miss Lancashire took my memory book that I was holding and started writing in it. I continued talking to the other students stood around us. Miss Lancashire gave me my book back.

"Have a good summer Maxine." I thanked her as she walked away to another group of students and I went to find Lauren and Darcy.

It was an emotional day, but I walked away from school knowing that in all my exams, I had done my absolute best. Lauren and Darcy were going on to college to study. I was going to stay on at school to do my A-levels, so that was our last day together. We had a great school life and we were just as close at the end as we were at the beginning. I was really looking forward to summer, I had lots planned, it was going to be one to remember.

When I think about how everything escalated since that fight with Lucy, I wonder if I should have seen it coming? Could I have avoided it? Would I really want to? Or was it always meant to be? We are reaching a point now where things are about to change, to take a new direction.

Chapter 9
Summer Holidays

A week after we broke up from school, I went on a two week holiday to Cyprus with my family. I didn't know at the time, but it would be the last holiday I would ever go on with them. It was amazing though. We had the best time, created so many memories. I remember where we stayed, it was like nothing I had ever seen before. It was a five-star hotel, on the outskirts of the main resort and only a five minute walk away from the beach.

Mum and Dad had their own room, and Chloe and I had the room next door. It was a twin but both beds were king-size. Chloe looked tiny in hers, it was really funny. Our room had big patio doors that looked out onto the sea. It was stunning. The hotel had three pools, and it's own restaurants and shops. I spent most of the time in the swimming pools. I adored swimming. Chloe and I spent a lot of time together that holiday too, just the two of us. We entered some dance competitions that the hotel entertainments team had put on. Chloe won one night and she was so happy. She always said she wanted to be a professional dancer, she had loads of potential. We also spent one afternoon at the beach on our own whilst Mum and Dad ate in the beach bar behind us. Chloe loved it when we were on our own, she felt like an adult. I got us some cherry mock-tails and she looked the perfect picture with her long brown hair and red sunglasses, sipping her drink. The weather was so hot too– Dad always tanned so well and so easy. Mum, Chloe and I tried to match Dad's tan but we never could.

    I am so grateful I got that time with Chloe to bond and make memories with her, and with my family. The chance to experience somewhere new with them will always be precious to me. I look back on that moment as a highlight of my entire life. I have a picture of us on that holiday next to my bed. Mum asked one of the ladies that worked in the hotel to take it for us. We were having dinner in the hotel, all dressed up. I think it was on our last night. Chloe and I had similar colour outfits on – I wore a brown jumpsuit and Chloe wore a brown dress. We had our hair curled, and I did our makeup. Dad wore a blue shirt that Mum had bought him with some black trousers, he looked very smart, especially with his glowy tan. Mum looked sensational. The most beautiful person I had ever seen. She wore a red dress, long and flowy and had a curly up-do. We all squeezed together for the photo laughing and joking, the picture captured the moment perfectly. We were the perfect family.

    A few days later we were back home in Manchester, and we'd brought the weather home with us. It was a beautiful, sunny day. I decided to sort through my work that I had brought home from school. I kept it in a brown box that was under my bed. I took the box and sat on my floor with it. I could hear Chloe in the garden playing with her friend who had come over. Mum had filled the paddling pool for them so I could hear them splashing about outside. I started looking through the box that was full of my projects, coursework, portfolios. The first thing that caught my eye was my memory book from school. I had forgot about it with us rushing off on holiday and all the stuff we'd needed to do to get ready for it. I must have just thrown it in the box on my last day and pushed it all under my bed. I remember a feeling of excitement as I laid the book out on my floor and got comfy, rolling onto my side to flip through the pages. I started reading through the messages. I remember the happy feeling I got looking at such lovely words that people wrote about me.

Good luck in everything you do, you are amazing, Ben.

Thanks for being my dance partner throughout the years, you are so talented and I hope you get all your dreams in life. Beth x

You are amazing and I know you are going to go on to do amazing things. Jessica xx

Thank you for all your hard work in my class, that smile of yours will get you far, Miss Lyons.

Such a nice girl, remember you cannot change the past only the future, go and get your dreams. Miss Adams.

Messages after messages, the pages of the book were overcrowded with positivity. I was about halfway through when I noticed a message from Miss Lancashire. I had forgot that in assembly on the last day she had written in it.

Maxine, it's been a pleasure, especially the past couple of months getting to know you. Good luck with your grades. I am sure I will see you on results day. Have a great summer, Miss Lancashire x

 It really touched me, it was a really nice message from her. I felt like I owed Miss Lancashire a lot. She really pushed me to do my best and went above and beyond for me. I wanted to make her proud. I took the book outside to show my parents. Mum loved reading all the messages, she said it was such a nice memento to be able to look back and reflect on. I got them to write something in it too, just for fun. It's hard for me to look back on that book now. It's in a small box on top of my wardrobe. I have days where I think about looking at it, reading it, remembering those times but it's too painful at the moment. Maybe one day I will.

 The night before I was going into school to get my results, I was so nervous. Mum made us her cheesy pasta dish but I struggled to eat it because I had knots in my stomach. I know I had tried my best but I kept expecting the worse. Mum and Dad told me to relax and to trust myself. Even Chloe was reassuring me, trying to calm me down. I remember the feeling of stress and panic I felt every time I imagined opening my results at school.

 Before bed, I decided to run myself a hot bubble bath. I soaked in the hot water for nearly two hours. The room was so steamy, I could barely see. The fruity bubble bath I used was filling the air. I also had candles sat around the outside of the bath to give it more of that spa atmosphere. I figured I needed it. I remember just closing my eyes and losing myself in the moment. Mum knocked on the door a few times, thinking I had drowned. She was joking of course, but I was in there a very long time.

    After my bath I messaged Lauren and Darcy. They were coming early the next day to my house so we could all go into school together. I got into bed and stared at the ceiling thinking about all the things that could happen, good and bad. I just wanted to get to school, get that envelope and see my grades. I put my phone on charge next to me and set my alarm. *I can do this*, I thought. *I can do this.*

Chapter 10
Results Day

    I knew the day ahead was going to be stressful, full of surprises for everyone involved. But I was not expecting or prepared for what was about to happen to me. If I had not gone into school on that day, if I would have had my results posted to me, then maybe things would have been different now. Maybe things would have been so very different.

    "Morning love." Mum walked into my room with a cup of tea.

    "How are you feeling?" Mum sat at the end of my bed offering support.

    "Scared." I said looking at my phone. Lauren had messaged me telling me that they were on their way and so I rushed around to get ready for them. When they arrived, Mum had made us some breakfast, and we all picked at it nervously. None of us spoke, we just stared at our plates, moving the food around with our forks.

    "I have never seen you three so quiet." Dad said as he walked through the kitchen into the conservatory to read his paper. Mum and Dad wished us luck as we left for the walk to school. When we arrived, there were some students sat outside, some looked happy, a few upset. Brown envelopes being opened everywhere. We walked into the reception area where the results were being given out. More students were in there already, some crying –

sad or happy tears, we did not know. Teachers were chatting, waiting for students and Miss Lancashire was making her way around everyone offering reassurance.
    We went to the reception desk and we all were given our brown envelopes. Lauren, Darcy and I looked at each other, hugged and went our separate ways. I took mine to the back of the art department. I sat on a bench and stared at this envelope that held a part of my future. I was nervous and anxious. After a while I quickly opened my envelope and scanned over my results. I got A's and B's across the board. I was ecstatic. I'd done it. I rang my parents who started shouting down the phone with excitement. I had a little cry and ran back to reception to Lauren and Darcy – they had done really well too. We all hugged and were congratulated by our teachers and other students. I felt a huge weight off my shoulders. Then I heard Miss Lancashire walk behind me.
    "Come to my office." Before I had chance to reply, she was walking away from me. I was feeling so happy with myself, for all of us. Everyone seemed so energised that day, it was nice to see people celebrating and it had broken down all the normal teacher-student boundaries and awkwardness. It was also eye-opening to see the disappointment on some students faces, realising they had blown it. I remember seeing Lucy in the midst of students – she read her results and ripped them up before throwing them in the bin. So I guessed that she did not do well. I was actually surprised that she even bothered showing up. We clocked each other before she left, no emotion, just eye contact. I watched her walk away. I was never going to see her again and I really was not bothered.

I walked away from the happy hustle and bustle of everyone to head to Miss Lancashire's office. I looked back and no one noticed me leave because everyone was wrapped up in the moment. I literally skipped down the corridor to her office, oblivious to everything else due to how happy I was. I knocked on her office door.

"Come in." I heard. Miss Lancashire stood with a cake, a large round chocolate cake.

"Congratulation's love." she said with a huge smile on her face.

"Do you do this for everyone?" I said more confidently.

"You did so well with your grades Maxine, you should be proud. Especially after your little blip, I'm glad that event didn't go too far and affect your final performance."

"How do you know what I got?"

"I got everyone's results last night and yours were the first I checked." It was quiet as we both stared at each other.

"Shall I take the cake back for everyone?" I asked. It was too much for me on my own, and it seemed unfair that I was the only one who got cake when everyone else had worked so hard as well.

"Can I do something Maxine?" I didn't know what she meant, but I nodded a little unsure. At this point I was stood in the middle of her office and she was stood by her desk holding the cake. She put the cake down and walked over to me. I thought about moving but I couldn't. My body froze. I didn't know why but the feeling in the room changed from relaxed and light-hearted to something more intense and serious. I remember my eyes starting to water, and my heart started beating really fast. Miss Lancashire came closer to me. I could smell her perfume, soft jasmine, mingling with the scent of lavender in the room.

"Miss, I think I should go." I mumbled.

"It's okay, I am not going to hurt you." She moved my hair from my face just like she did in art class. I looked away from her. I knew this wasn't right. I hoped that someone would come in, another teacher or even a student. But no one did. She moved closer and put my face in her hands, making me look at her. I could feel her coming closer to me. I did not move away. I did not do anything. I just stared into her eyes. She pulled me in, our lips touched and before I knew it, we kissed.

I was lost in the moment, a good or bad moment, I didn't know. After a few seconds, she pulled away from me.

"I'm sorry Maxine." she said rushing back to her desk. I stood not knowing what to do or where to look.

"Come here love, sit down." She ushered me towards the chair. I stood and shook my head. She walked back over to me.

"Give me your phone love." I took my phone out of my pocket, unlocked it in a state of shock and gave it to her. She tapped the screen, putting in her personal phone number, under the name **friend**.

"Text me later please." She handed me the cake and showed me to the door.

"You don't tell anyone about this." she said as she closed the door behind me. I stood in the corridor holding the cake she had given me. I could feel myself shaking. I stood looking around. I was waiting for someone to see

me, for me to see someone. I looked at Miss Lancashire's office door and thought about going back in. I stood there for a good five minutes in my own world, trying to make sense of what had just happened. Eventually I made my way back to the reception area in a daze. I put the cake down on a random table. Lauren looked over to me.
"That's from Miss Lancashire, isn't it?"
"No." I snapped. A few other people asked where I got it from, but I quickly brushed past the subject saying my parents just gave it to me. I needed some air. I felt like I couldn't breathe. I went and sat on the grass at the back of the school field. It was peaceful there. It was so warm I could feel the heat on my entire body. You could see houses from the field, their back gardens looked onto the school. I remember seeing families in their gardens enjoying the sun, children playing with each other. It took my mind off what happened for a few seconds. What did happen? I suddenly thought. Should I tell someone? Lauren or Darcy? My mum? I knew that she shouldn't have done what she did. But I never pulled away. I never did anything. I let it happen.

    I got myself together and made my way back to reception. It was much quieter, some of the other students had left. The cake had nearly all gone too. I looked for Lauren and Darcy but Miss Smith who worked in reception told me they had left. I could not believe they had gone home and not told me. I did have messages from them asking me what was wrong and where I was, but I did not see them until later.

    I took some of the cake and sat on a chair. It looked and smelt delicious, but I couldn't bring myself to eat any of it. I sat there for a bit and then got up to leave.

"Bye Miss." I said to Miss Smith. I started walking down the school drive but I couldn't get Miss Lancashire out of my head. Before I got to the school gate I turned around and went back into school. I didn't have a plan. I didn't know what I was doing. But I knew it did not feel right to leave. I rushed back to Miss Lancashire's office and knocked on her door. I didn't even know if she would still be at school. The door opened; Miss Lancashire stood- shocked to see me.

"Oh hello, you better come in." She held the door open for me, and I walked nervously past her. I was standing in the same place where I stood previously. She closed the door and stood in front of it.

Silence.

I knew what I was thinking but I couldn't get the words out at first. I had one question to ask her. Just one. After a few minutes I decided to ask.

"Will you kiss me again?" I said looking at the floor, wishing it would swallow me whole.

"What?" Miss Lancashire looked confused. I did not say anything else. After a moment's pause, she walked over to me and put her hand under my chin to direct my attention to hers. I remember closing my eyes, waiting for the moment to happen again. After a few seconds, I felt it. Her lips on mine. It was not just a quick kiss that time, it lasted longer. I had never felt like that before, like I had this ball of excitement in my stomach. I don't know why I asked her to kiss me again, but I did not want her to stop. A few seconds went past, and she pulled away once more.

"Are you okay?" she said concerned.
"I don't know what's happening Miss."
"I would never hurt you Maxine, you know that don't you?"
"I need to go." I rushed out of her office.

When I got home, Mum and Dad had done a buffet for me. They had also decorated the house. Huge pink balloons were tied to our front gate and when I walked through the door, they all rushed to congratulate me. Chloe jumped on me screaming. I burst out crying realising what had just happened at school.
"Aww, darling." Mum said hugging me. Dad also came over.
"Come on love, you can have some champagne, time to celebrate." Obviously, my parents thought I was overwhelmed with my results but they were the last thing on my mind. I followed them into the kitchen. There was a beautiful cake that Mum had bought for me. It was red velvet. It had the family picture on from when we went to Cyprus and in pink icing it said,
We are so proud of you xxx
They also gave me a small gift bag. I looked inside and there was a black box with a red bow on it. I opened it and inside was a silver bracelet with my birthstone attached to it. It was stunning. I told them how much I loved them and thanked them for being there for me. I will keep that bracelet until the day I die. It's my most valued item. It was then, and it still is now.
That night I looked at my phone drafting messages to send to Miss Lancashire. I kept thinking that she might not want me to message her anymore, she might have

changed her mind. Changed her mind about what? I thought. I started answering my own questions in a bit of a panic. After an hour of drafting things to say and talking myself out of texting, I sent her a message.

Maxine
Thanks for the cake! Maxine x.

    I put my phone quickly on my bedside table like it was going to explode and I laid in bed waiting. I kept checking the door thinking someone was going to walk in at any moment and take my phone away. After a few minutes my phone buzzed. It was Miss Lancashire. It took me a while to open the message.

Friend
No problem love x

    We started texting from that night. Just casual messages about our days, what we were doing in the holidays. We messaged a lot. It almost became routine. Then one night a message read,

Friend
What you doing tomorrow, you want to go for a drive?

    I felt my heart beat harder, butterflies in my stomach, making me feel a bit queasy. I grasped my phone smiling.

Maxine
Yes x

Friend
Great, I will pick you up at 10, end of your road. Goodnight Maxine x

    I had been waiting for that message for so long but now it was there in front of me. I was scared. I sometimes thought about messaging her to meet but I could never bring myself to do it.

Chapter 11
Out Of Hours

    I had not seen Miss Lancashire since results day, so I was anxious but I did want to see her again. I went into Mum's room that night and made some excuse about going into town to pick up some clothes for my A-levels. She even gave me some money to treat myself. I sat with her in bed while we had a girly chat, there was a chick flick movie on in the background. She asked me if I wanted her to go shopping with me but I told her I was okay and wanted to have a browse on my own. I felt guilty lying to everyone but especially Mum. We had a laugh that night about this and that. I paused in the moment just watching her laugh. She's proper beautiful, my mum.
"I love you." I said as I wrapped my arms around her.
"I love you too babe."
I spent that night choosing a nice dress to wear. I decided to put on my denim long sleeve dress, it was one of my favourites. Mum bought it for my fifteenth birthday. I thought it made me look grown up. I didn't really sleep much that night. I was very restless with anticipation.

    It was a lovely morning, warm and sunny. I left home with my family who were having a lie-in, oblivious to what I was doing, who I was meeting, what had happened a few weeks before. I walked to the end of my street. I could see Miss Lancashire's big silver car already parked up around the corner, hidden by large bushes and trees that filled our street. I could see her smiling at me before I got to her.

"Hiya Miss." I said as I got into her car. She handed me a chocolate milkshake that she had picked up for me beforehand.

"You don't have to call me Miss now." She laughed. Miss Lancashire looked so glamorous, not at all like she did at school. Her hair was wavy, she had a floral long top on over some black skinny jeans, and she was wearing black heels with black shades on her head.

"You can call me Jane."

"Okay."

"You feel okay?"

"Yeah, I'm good."

It was a little strange at first, but I soon felt very relaxed with her. She drove us out of town, and pulled up at the top of a hill that looked out onto the city. It was beautiful. There were a few people on the hill side, some having a picnic, some walking their dogs, all relaxing and enjoying the sun. Miss Lancashire opened her boot and got out a blanket and some treats that she had picked up for us.

We talked for hours, getting to know each other on a personal level. She told me she went to university and became a teacher almost straight away, working her way up. She had a couple of relationships but none of them ever lasted. She was not close to her family because they did not approve of her lifestyle choice. I did not ask her what she meant by that, but I figured she meant liking women rather than men. The conversation quickly turned to what happened in her office. Miss Lancashire moved and sat behind me, resting her head on my shoulder. The mood became serious. I did not like how it felt in that moment. I felt like she was proving a point, that she had the power and she was the one in control.

"What happened at school should not have happened."

"I know, but I wanted it to." I insisted.

"You can never tell anyone Maxine."

"I know, I wouldn't."

"Students and teachers should not do what we are doing."

"I know, I promise I won't say anything." Miss Lancashire ran her fingers through my hair, then she used it to gently but firmly pull me back into her, so I was leaning in her lap.

"Where did you tell your parents you were going?"

"Into town to pick up some new clothes."

"Good, let's go shopping then." Miss Lancashire stood up, kissing me on the head as she did. It was an unusual moment but I figured she needed to be sure of a few things. We packed up the car not long after and she drove us to a shopping outlet. I had passed it a few times with Mum but had never gone into it before. She told me to pick out what I liked. I remember filling the basket up with tops, skirts, pants, bags, shoes, lots of accessories. Miss Lancashire bought them all for me. It must have been well over £100,00. I was so grateful and I did not expect it. I had my own money from my mum but she wanted to treat me and she would not let me pay.

"Right, I better get you back home Missy." I didn't want to go home but I knew she was right. We stopped a few streets away. I took off my seat belt and turned to face her.

"Thank you for today." I said a little giddy.
She leaned in and kissed me on the forehead.

"I'll message you later." I walked home happy and content.

My mum was in the living room when I got in and was amazed at how much I had bought. I said they were all in the sales to avoid suspicion. I couldn't stop smiling. I'd had the best day, despite the chat that had been a little intense. I thought at least that was done with now.

We had a BBQ that night too with family and friends. Darcy and Lauren came around with their parents. We had spoken since results day and had sorted everything out, so we were now back in a good place. I told them that Miss Lancashire did give me the cake, but it was for everyone. I also told them that the reason why I disappeared was because I was overwhelmed and needed some alone time. They seemed to buy it and nothing more was said.

After the picnic, Miss Lancashire would often pick me up at the end of my road, or just around the corner so her car was always hidden by the large trees. She would drive us out of the city, places I had never been before or even heard off. Usually on the outskirts so it would be safer. I remember when she took me to some small country pub for a meal, we ended up getting a taxi together because she wanted to have a few drinks. It was called *The Lost Lamb;* it was tiny and we were the only people there. We sat outside, looking out onto acres of land. We had red wine that she ordered. I had never drunk wine before. Mum and Dad let me have shandy and the

occasional champagne on special occasions, but they were always there watching me- making sure I wasn't having too much and getting silly. I felt very grown up on my own with Miss Lancashire. The bartender didn't know I was drinking because she bought me juice to drink too. It was a little bit sneaky, but we only had one bottle and she drank more than me because I found the wine hard to drink, especially at first. She kept staring at me, saying how grown up I looked and then out of nowhere she blurted out,
    "Maxine, I'm thirty five." I paused for a moment taking in what she had said.
    "Does that bother you?" she asked. I reassured her that I knew what I was doing, what we were doing, what this was. I might have been young, but I was not stupid. I wanted it to happen. If I didn't then I would have said something. It was something we were aware of but when I was with her, I never really thought about it. It was not a priority. I was going to be sixteen soon anyway and then age-wise it wouldn't even be that bad, would it? I know you're probably thinking that it definitely is bad. That I was being naive, that I was being groomed – but I really wasn't. If I wanted to walk away, then I could. I just didn't want to.
    A few days before my sixteenth birthday, I got a text from Lauren saying her and Darcy wanted to meet me for coffee. The message was pretty casual, so I did not think anything of it. When I arrived at our usual coffee shop, they were already sat at a table. I could tell there was some underlying tension from the way they did not smile at me when I walked in. And the way they kept looking at each other like they were anticipating something.

"What's happened?" I asked, nervously. They were being weird, and I felt on edge. Darcy looked over at Lauren who decided to finally speak to me.

"What is going on with you and Miss Lancashire?"

"What do you mean?"

"We saw you with her, in her car." My heart sank. They couldn't have, we were so careful.

"Oh, I bumped into her in town the other day, I felt sick, so she took me home." Lauren and Darcy looked confused, not believing what I was telling them.

"You were laughing in her car, I saw you near school at the traffic lights." Lauren insisted, not satisfied by my lies. I knew exactly what she was talking about, she must have spotted us when Miss Lancashire was taking me home from one of our dates. I could not tell them the truth. I couldn't do it. I took a breath.

"I don't know what you think you're accusing me of. It was by accident that we bumped into each other. There is nothing to worry about."

"First she lets you skip class, makes you tea, gives you cake and now you're meeting her outside of school." Her tone was accusing. I looked at Lauren in shock at what she had said to me. I glanced at Darcy who was finding the chat uncomfortable and wouldn't make eye contact with me. I stood up defiantly.

"I do not need to justify a teacher being nice to me. Get over it." I headed for the door in a panic.

"Don't be like that." I heard from behind me, but I carried on and did not look back. On my way home, I thought about what I was going to do. I decided not to tell Miss Lancashire because it might have caused concern which I did not want, but my birthday was coming up, so I needed to make up with Lauren and Darcy. I needed them on side. That night I sent them a message in our group chat.

Maxine: *Hey, sorry about today, I just felt a bit ambushed. Nothing's happened, honestly.*
Lauren: *It's fine, we were just worried.*
Darcy: *We don't want to fall out, we love you, we just wanted to make sure you were okay.*
Maxine: *I love you too, let's just leave it. I can't wait for my birthday, you decided what to wear yet?*

I had to be careful, no one could know what I was doing. No one.

Chapter 12
Sweet Sixteen

"Happy Birthday to you, Happy Birthday to you, Happy Birthday to Maxine, Happy Birthday to you." Chloe rushed into my bedroom jumping on my bed.
"I love you." she said cuddling up to me.
"I love you too cutie." It was 8.00AM, the morning of my sixteenth birthday. We were having a huge house party that afternoon, family, friends, people from school. The first thing I thought about when I woke up was Miss Lancashire. I tried not to but I couldn't help it. I could not get her out of my head. I checked my phone and I had plenty of messages from family and friends wishing me happy birthday. But the only message I wanted to see was one from Miss Lancashire. I scrolled through everything until I found it.

Friend
Happy Birthday beautiful! See you later x

I could not wait to see her. Chloe and I went downstairs. Mum and Dad were in the living room sat on the sofa having a cuppa, snuggled in their PJ's.
"Happy Birthday love." Mum rushed up and gave me a hug.
"We didn't expect you to be up yet." Dad said, kissing me on the cheek.

"I wanted a sleep in but someone had other ideas." I said, nudging my sister. Chloe started laughing and ushered me to the fireplace. There were presents in a pile wrapped in shiny pink paper and each one had a pink bow on it.
"You can open these now, more to come later." Dad said, smiling at Mum and looking very pleased with himself. I sat in front of the fire and started working my way through the presents. I was truly spoiled. I got perfume, earrings, clothes, chocolates, money. I was so grateful to my parents, they always went above and beyond. My whole birthday morning was very relaxed, lots of lounging around, being waited on by my parents. I could not wait to see everyone at my party. It wouldn't be long before we were starting back at school and college, so it was the last big get-together for all of us before we went our separate ways. At around 11.30AM I got another message from Miss Lancashire asking me to try and get away for the full night. She had a surprise for me. I didn't know if I would be able to stay the night with her, but I told her I would try my best.

I remember my sixteenth birthday like it was yesterday, it's crazy to think that it was three years ago now. How time flies. The guests were due at 5.00PM, but I couldn't wait any longer and as soon as it got to 3.00PM, I started getting ready. Mum had booked me a hair and make-up artist, which was a welcomed and exciting surprise. I had never had my make-up done professionally before, so I couldn't wait for her to arrive. Dad left us in the house to get ready whilst he sorted all the garden out so that it was a man-free zone. We had music playing, we were drinking fruit punches that Mum had made, it was really special. We were having the best time, laughing and joking in our robes.

My birthday outfit was stunning – Mum had helped me pick it out from a designer shop in town. It was a loose pink sparkly dress with silver shoes. I had my hair in loose curls, black smokey eyes with a pink lip and a golden shimmery tan. I felt on top of the world. I remember looking into the landing mirror before heading downstairs and being taken back by how grown up I looked. I could have passed for twenty, easily. I could hear friends and family interacting with each other as I walked into the living room and conservatory area. Everyone looked at me and clapped, hugging and kissing me, wishing me happy birthday. Everyone said how beautiful and grown up I looked. Lauren and Darcy came over to me. We hugged like we had never hugged before. I loved those girl's so much, even to this day I still call them my best friends.

My party started in the house and then moved into the garden area, my parents set up a gazebo in the garden with karaoke which we all loved and got involved with. It was such a hot day, the perfect weather for a party. I wasn't allowed to drink proper alcohol, my dad would say, but they made an exception for my birthday. I had a glass of champagne at the start and they made an alcoholic punch, some alcoholic cocktails and we could drink some cider. I think because the party was full of family and friends, everyone looked out for each other. And even though I felt responsible and grown up, the adults were definitely keeping tabs.

Later on in the evening after everyone had sang happy birthday, my parents came over to me with an envelope. They had bought me driving lessons ready for when I was seventeen. I was thrilled, Dad then took my hand and walked me through the house to the front drive. Mum, Chloe and a few others followed. I stood at the front of our house looking around.

"Happy Birthday darling. I know you can't drive it yet, but this was always your dream when you were little." Dad handed me some keys. I looked at our driveway with my Mum and Dad's car there, I could not see anything else. I pressed the keys and lights flashed to the side. I looked at where the lights were coming from and gasped, hugging my dad. They had bought me a car. I couldn't believe it. A pale pink Mini stood near our house; it was perfect. I sat in it honking the horn, so pleased – by that point everyone had gathered outside the front of our house, taking pictures and videos of me and the car. Mum said I had to stop because it would annoy the neighbours but we were all laughing and joking and come to think of it most of the neighbours were at our house anyway.

"You're only sixteen once." Dad shouted. Chloe bought me a *Pandora* bracelet with some charms; a number sixteen, a love heart and a sister charm. Lauren and Darcy got me a spa day for three, and I got flowers and chocolate from everyone else. I had a fabulous cake too, it was shaped like a camera and my favourite flavour- red velvet. Everything was pink and silver. Mum had done an amazing job making sure everything matched and complemented each other. I had the best day, the best family. It was just perfect. I just wished Miss Lancashire could have been there to experience it with me, but I knew it could never happen.

The party went well and gradually everyone made their way home. I was slightly tipsy if I am honest. I was not used to drinking and I did manage to drink quite a bit.

It was around 9.00PM when I asked Mum and Dad if I could go out with some friends, they said yes after a while of talking them round. We had decided to go back to Jess' house, she was not a close friend but we all got on and her parents had an amazing house. I had been to her house once before and loved it. At my party, Jess said that her parents would put the hot tub on for us, if we wanted to go around for a few hours. There were eight girl's there including Lauren, Darcy and I that jumped at the chance. Secretly, I had other ideas and messaged Miss Lancashire straight away to tell her the plan.

We all made our way outside to wait for the taxis we had ordered. None of the adults could drive us because they'd all had too much to drink. They decided to stay on at my house and have some adult time.

"I will catch you guys up later." I said. Lauren and Darcy looked at me suspiciously.

"Where are you going?" Darcy said.

"I just want to thank my parents again."

"You're not going to meet her, are you?" Lauren said shaking her head. I laughed.

"Stop it, of course I'm not. I will see you in a bit."

"Maxine, seriously." Lauren shook her head at Darcy.

"Please don't ruin tonight for me." I kissed them on the cheek and waved them off in the taxi. I waited until it was out of sight. I felt rubbish lying because I knew I had no intention of going back. I just wanted to go and see Miss Lancashire. I made my way around the corner to Miss Lancashire's car. Her eyes gleamed when she saw me.

"Wow, you look amazing." I smiled and got in. I don't think she could believe how grown up I looked.

"Where are we going?"

"It's a surprise." I stared out of the window at all the houses we passed, all the people enjoying the last of the sun. I looked over to Miss Lancashire driving, daydreaming of how perfect everything felt.

"Maxine, can I ask you something?"

"What is it?"

"Do you feel safe with me?"

"Yeah, I do."

"Good, that's good." She held my hand tight and drove us to a luxury apartment block. I followed her into a glass, brightly lit building. We went up to the third floor and she opened a door with a number sixteen on it. It was absolutely stunning inside. Everything was cream and glittery. There were gifts on the luxury, silk double bed. I went over to them – teddies, chocolate, flowers, a designer watch. I was truly spoiled and felt very overwhelmed. I could not believe she would do all that for me.

"I booked it for the night."

"It really is beautiful, thank you." Miss Lancashire went into the bathroom. I sat down at the dressing table. I could see Miss Lancashire's reflection in the bathroom through the mirror. She was so beautiful. She ran her hand through her blonde curly hair, touched up her lipstick and sprayed herself with her perfume. She caught me staring at her in the mirror and smiled at me. She turned off the bathroom light and walked over to me. She stood behind me, running her fingers through my hair.

"This is nice, here with you." I said. I could feel my body start to shiver. She kissed me on the head and slowly unbuttoned my top staring at me in the mirror as she did. I stared back before looking up at her. She leaned over me, her hand grabbing my hair holding my head to hers. We kissed. She put her other hand on my face and started kissing my cheek and neck.

"Come with me." she whispered into my ear.

"I can't stay the night; my friends and family are expecting me back soon." I said disappointed.

"They have had you all day, now it's my turn." she said cuddling up to me. I could hear my phone going off as she led me to the bed but I ignored it. Nothing else mattered.

"Happy Birthday, darling."

Chapter 13
First Time

    I knew what was going to happen. All these feelings rushed through my body. I felt on fire. I know that it should not have got that far with Miss Lancashire. Trust me. I know that student and teachers should not be like that with each other. But I was in this bubble. I felt safe. I felt secure. I felt like nothing else mattered. I sat down on the bed, she knelt in front of me and started taking my dress off revealing my underwear. She put her arms around me to unfasten my bra, feeling my breasts as she pushed me back onto the bed. She moved her hands down my body, taking off my knickers. She stood and leaned over me on the bed.
    "You're trembling." she whispered. She took my hands and held them above my head. Slowly she started kissing my neck, my chest, all the way down, no place was left untouched. She let go of my hands and held my neck, not hard enough so it hurt but hard enough so I couldn't move my head. She put her tongue in my mouth and the kissing got faster and faster. I grasped the sheets.
    "My angel." Our eyes made contact, she moved one hand down my body. I felt a sharp pain at first and then slowly the pain started to go as she moved her hand inside of me. I had never experienced anything like that before. I didn't want it to end. Do you ever feel an emotion so strong, so powerful it overwrites all common sense? All

normality? If you died in that moment, you would die completely happy, fulfilled, content? That's what it felt like for me.

I remember staring at the ceiling. It seemed to move; I could hear my heart beating in my chest. Miss Lancashire put her arm around me. She cuddled me so tight. I felt myself drift off. It was suddenly black.

"Maxine." I felt my arm been moved. I slowly woke up to Miss Lancashire sat next to me on the bed.

"Wake up love, it's almost midnight."

"What?" I said panicking. I jumped up and grabbed my phone. I had so many missed calls from Lauren and Darcy and my mum. I glanced at my reflection in the mirror and I remember how bad I looked, my makeup was smudged, my hair a mess and my lovely dress was creased. Miss Lancashire helped me sort myself out and gathered my things together. I was gutted I had to leave, but I could not stay the night.

"I had a great time; this place is stunning." I told her breathlessly, she smiled and hugged me tight. We made our way downstairs to her car.

That night when I finally got home, my family were really worried. I had never seen them so worried. They were waiting up when I made my way through the door. I walked into the hallway.

"She's here, alright, thank you." Mum put down the phone.

"Where the hell have you been?"

"Sorry, I lost track of time."

"Well, you weren't at Jess' house, because I have spoken to Lauren and Darcy, so where have you been?"

"I went to Bea's house, she text me wanting to give me some presents." I showed Mum the gift bag full of the gifts that Miss Lancashire had given me. Dad came from the conservatory.

"Chrissie, let's leave it until tomorrow."

"I just got carried away and fell asleep, you can ring Bea's mum if you don't believe me." I knew they wouldn't bother, not at that time.

"You make sure you at least text us next time." Dad said as he followed Mum upstairs.

"Thank you for a fabulous birthday. I love you both!" I called after them.

I sat with Chloe for a bit in her room before I made my way to bed. She was asleep but I laid with her for a while. I did have an argument that night with Lauren and Darcy on messenger. They said I needed to stop lying to them and that they knew something was going on. They told me how disappointed they were in me. I knew they were worried about me but I told them they needed to back off. That I should be allowed other friends. The argument did not last long. I told them that we were all changing and if they did not like it then maybe we should take a break. They quickly reacted and clearly the arguing had got to them. They apologised and said they were just worried when I went off for hours. I told them I got distracted with Bea and fell asleep. I messaged Bea and asked her if she would back me up, she was not sure at first but she could tell I was desperate and agreed.

Bea was someone I got on well with at school. We had a laugh but we were never really close. We went out for lunch sometimes, and she had slept at my house before. But it was a more casual friendship. We were not in each other's pockets. My parents never rang Bea's mum to check my story. They decided to trust me, and I was grateful.

    After that night in the apartment, I felt myself change. It was frustrating for me. I wanted to tell my family and friends that I had sex. I wanted to tell them how amazing it was. But I couldn't tell anyone. I was alone in my thoughts. I really wanted to tell Lauren and Darcy. I used to imagine myself giggling when telling them all the details, trying to get the words out. I imagined how they would tease me, but they would want to know. They would want to be part of it. It would have been nice, one of those best friend moments that stays with you forever. When we were all fifty, I imagined us reminiscing about it, drinking wine, being happy. But I knew that would never be. So, I had those moments alone in my head.
    There were only a few weeks left of the summer. I could feel myself drifting away from friends and family, so I decided to spend the rest of the summer with them. It was nice, family meals and get-togethers. Shopping and day trips with the girl's. We still had good times, but I guess things just seemed a little different. I felt myself kind of acting because my mind was always somewhere else. I figured they would sense that. The person that I was showing everyone was not the person I was inside, because inside all I could think about was Miss Lancashire. I was obsessed.

A few days before I was due to start back at school, Miss Lancashire messaged me to meet. She picked me up at the end of the street and drove us to a tea room in a garden centre. She asked me if I was ready to get back into my studies and if there was anything I needed. I already had everything because Mum had got me stocked up on all things educational. I thanked her again for my birthday and told her what an amazing time I had. How I could not stop thinking about it and how much I wanted to do it again. Miss Lancashire smiled but it seemed awkward, like she wanted me to stop talking about it. I asked if she was okay and she said that everything was fine. I went quiet not knowing what to say. She asked for the bill and we left. The journey home was much better, we had a laugh.

"Sorry love." Miss Lancashire put her hand on my leg.

"I've just got a lot on with school starting again."

"It's okay, I understand." That was the last time I saw her during the holidays, she started taking ages to respond to my messages and when she did, her replies were brief. I had no idea what was going on and the worst part was there was nobody I could talk to about it. No one at all.

Chapter 14
A-levels

Monday morning, the summer was over. I did have a great summer that year but a lot was going on, a lot of things that I could not control. I was really looking forward to getting back to school to do my A-levels, to have some normality back in my life. My plan was still on track to go to university to study fashion. I just needed to keep my head down and work hard. I decided to continue with art, dance and media studies at A-level along with English.

The first day back was an introduction into how the next couple of years would work. There were some returning students who I knew and some new students who all seemed nice. Sixth Form was good because you could go into school to do the subjects you wanted – there was much more freedom in terms of working at home and at school. It felt very professional and I was ready for the challenge. This was the next chapter in getting to where I always wanted to go. I could not afford to mess it up. Towards the end of my first day, I was in the A-level canteen finishing off some study plans for my modules. Miss Lancashire opened the door and called across the room to me.

"Maxine, can I have a word?" I had not seen or spoken to her in a few days and I remember feeling nervous at the way she stood staring at me. Her hands on her hips, her eyes looking over the rim of her glasses, leaning against the door and urging me to go with her. A few dinner ladies looked over to me and smiled. I think they felt sorry for me. I got my things together in my bag and followed her into her office. She opened the door for me to walk in first.

"Just take a...sit down."

"This is very formal." I said. Miss Lancashire sat down behind her desk and took a moment to pause before she spoke.

"I am very fond of you, you know that. I just don't think I can do this anymore. We can be friends but the other thing, I'm just not ready to go there. You're so young Maxine, and I don't want to patronise you but I need to put you first." I sat there in disbelief. I could feel my eyes start to water but I was determined not to break down. It was silent. I did not understand. We had done so much together. I needed to leave before she saw me getting upset.

"I've got to go see Mrs Davis about my schedule." I rushed to go.

"Lucky you." Miss Lancashire said with a slight smile. I think she was trying to be funny, but she was not making me laugh.

"I'm sorry." she said, my back to her. Before I opened the door to leave, I looked at her, tears started to fall.

"Yeah, me too." I left her office and headed to find Mrs Davis.

Mrs Davis was the A-level programme co-ordinator. She always wore black trouser suits and bold colour blouses- she was very smart. She must have been in her fifties, brown hair that was always down and was blow-dried to perfection. I had seen her around school and occasionally engaged in a few conversations. She was always bubbly and pleasant. But I felt sick to my stomach as I made my way to her office. I went to see Mrs Davis to discuss my preferred A-level subjects because some of them clashed time-wise, so she had invited me to her office to hopefully come up with a solution.

When I saw Mrs Davis, she could tell that I had been crying. She asked if I was okay and I just said that I was overwhelmed with so much going on. We worked out a timetable that suited everyone and I was pleased I could take all the subjects that I wanted. I was excited at the beginning of that day and by the end I felt rubbish. Nothing made sense. Nothing at all. I felt like I had lost part of who I was, part of me felt broken and I did not know how to fix it.

Over the next few days, I started settling into A-level life. The work had not really started yet, so it was easy. I only had four courses to do so at that moment I had lots of free time. One dinner time I was sat in the canteen alone. I did not notice Mrs Finn in the dinner queue but when I did, I smiled at her and she smiled back. Mrs Finn was one of those teachers who really cared for her students in and out of school. I trusted her and appreciated her always going out of her way to make sure I was okay. She came over to me. I must have looked upset.

"Can I join you?" she asked.
"I don't think I will be much company."
"Anything you want to talk about?" I looked at her and I thought about the question for some time. I wanted to talk to someone so much. I needed to. Sometimes I felt

like I was losing my mind, on my own with all these thoughts.
"Miss, can I ask you something?"
"Yes Maxine, what is it?" she said waiting for my response. I clutched my clammy hands and took a breath. That night as soon as I got in, I messaged Miss Lancashire.

Maxine
I might have told Mrs Finn by accident.

I waited all night for a reply which never came. The next day I was stood outside of the photography room, waiting to be let in. I heard Miss Lancashire before I saw her walking towards me. She looked furious.
"Walk." She gestured for me to walk alongside her. Other students walked past but I felt alone in a hostile bubble.
"So you might have told Mrs Finn? What did you say?"
"I was upset, I was sat in the canteen. Mrs Finn came over to me."
"Yes and what did you say to her?"
"She asked me what was wrong. I said I had been seeing someone and that I had been dumped, but I accidentally said 'she' instead of 'he' and she asked if it was someone from school." She stopped us in the corridor.
"Did you say my name?"
"No." I said quietly. "Are you cross?". Miss Lancashire walked away from me like I was an

inconvenience. I know I wasn't her priority any more but I still had feelings. I shouted after her.

"You know what? Maybe I will tell her." A burst of confidence rushed through my body. Miss Lancashire turned back to me, grabbing my arm as she shoved me to a quieter part of the corridor.

"You see Maxine, this is the reason I can't do this anymore. Because you clearly can't handle the real world. Do not start something you cannot finish. Now get back to your class." I ran away from her crying. I just wanted to go home. I hated her. I never wanted to see her again.

I could not believe it. I had worked so hard to get to this level of my education, my A-levels had not even started properly yet and already I did not want to be at school. Nothing made sense any more, not when Miss Lancashire wasn't okay with me. I felt like I was carrying a massive weight on my shoulders. I isolated myself in the study room and tried to get on with the rest of my day. Before the school day was over, Miss Lancashire text me asking if she could meet me in the park. I wasn't sure about meeting her but she was very persistent.

At 5.30PM, I sat down on a bench hidden by overgrown graves, overgrown trees and bushes and waited with anticipation. The park was opposite the front field of the school. It was attached to an old cemetery, so it was quiet. The people that went there were always in their own world, no one cared what anyone else was doing. A few minutes went by and I could see Miss Lancashire in the distance. I had that sickly feeling again the closer she got to me.

"I am sorry for how I spoke to you Maxine." Miss Lancashire sat next to me on the bench.
"What happened? You made my birthday so special. I don't understand what changed."
"Maxine, I do appreciate what we did. But you are a child, technically you are a student in my school, none of it should have happened."
"But..."
"No buts, you need your education. I won't be a distraction. I still want to be a friend to you, if you'll let me?"
"Did you ever like me?"
"Of course I did. Come here." I did not move as she wrapped her arms around me. I could smell her perfume, soft jasmine. I remember closing my eyes and just appreciating the moment. She pulled away and offered me a lift home. I told her I was okay and walked away from her. I decided on that walk home that I was going to focus on my A-levels. I only had two years to get through and then I could move on and start again. I was upset but what else could I do? I had no control over anything. I just needed to focus on my goal.

I messaged Lauren and Darcy to see if they wanted to do something. I needed cheering up. We met in town and went to an Italian restaurant. It had just opened in the area. It was always nice to see them, but the feeling had definitely changed when we were together. The thing is, when you're so close with people that know you better than you know yourself, it is hard to have and keep secrets.

"Maxine, what is it?" Lauren reached for my hand over the table.

"What do you mean? I'm fine"
"Babe, you barely touched your food, something is wrong." Darcy moved closer to me. I looked at both of them in the eyes and I could see the concern they had for me. I did not want to lie, but I could not tell the truth. I shook my head and tried to reassure them I was fine, but I could not hold back the tears. I broke down on the table. It was too much for me. I couldn't handle not being with Miss Lancashire. Lauren and Darcy came and stayed with me that weekend and they really made an effort to cheer me up. They tried so many times to get me to open up, but I knew they wouldn't fully understand even if they wanted too. It did help being with them though. It was like old times, young and carefree.

    A few weeks later I was in the dance studio, finishing one of my dance routines that I was choreographing myself. I stayed over lunch to practice. The workload was beginning to slowly pile up and the work was getting more and more demanding. I liked the people in my modules but I was not close to anyone. I mostly kept myself to myself. I had definitely changed a lot since my GCSEs. I used to be so bubbly and outgoing, popular and always a leader in the pack. During my A-levels I spent a lot of time studying on my own. It was not a bad thing; it was just different.
    I was midway through my routine when I looked in the back mirror. I could see Miss Lancashire stood behind me. I stopped, the music still playing.
    "Can I talk to you?"
    "I guess." Miss Lancashire walked closer to me. I backed off.

"Okay, so I'm scared. Don't look like that Maxine. This, us, people won't get it. You know it's wrong don't you? Fuck!" I had never heard her swear before, I could tell this was hard on her. But in my head, I did not understand how something that felt so right could be so wrong. Miss Lancashire put her head in her hands. I watched her for a moment.

"Do you regret it? Kissing me?" I said.

"No. I probably should but I don't. I can't stop thinking about you. This could end my career. People will say I took advantage, call me a paedophile. And I am not that. I just... I won't let that happen but I won't lose you either."

"Miss, I don't know what you want from me."

"Let's go away for the weekend soon, just us?"

"Really?" I was surprised at her suggestion so suddenly.

"I'll sort it, I think it will be good for us." Miss Lancashire left the dance studio, clearly upset. I turned the music off and sat on the floor, exhausted and confused. I could hear my heart beating. I really liked her. I liked her so much that it was starting to physically hurt.

Chapter 15
Weekend Away

    Miss Lancashire and I started texting more after the chat we had in dance. It was back to some sort of normal, whatever that was. We started planning our trip away together. But we didn't see each other outside of school much because I was busy with coursework and so was she. She was always at meetings and training days; she had a busy life. I tried to keep in contact with Lauren and Darcy, arranging days out together. We were trying to keep our friendship alive, but we were all becoming different people. I don't think they trusted me anymore.
    Miss Lancashire called me into her office one day after school to show me a place she had found. It looked amazing, a hotel near Halifax. Miss Lancashire only showed me the front of the brochure. I think she wanted it to be a surprise.
    "How about we go next weekend?"
    "I just need to tell my parents something but yes! I can't wait."
    That night I told Mum and Dad that I had been invited to go away for the weekend with one of my new friends and their parents. They seemed uncertain and wanted me to get contact numbers from the made-up parents in case of emergencies. Which was understandable but of course impossible. I ended up making up a number to give them and reminding them that

I was not a child and wanted to be trusted. After a while they gave in and gave their permission. I text Miss Lancashire straight away. I thought that going away together meant we could be ourselves, to not have to pretend to be something else, but I was wrong.

Friday evening, it was around 5.00PM. I stayed at school until Miss Lancashire had finished in her meetings. I was daydreaming in the study room where Miss Lancashire had told me to wait for her. I thought back to my first time in her office, when I had that fight with Lucy Blackmore. I could not believe how things had changed since then. I had my little bag packed, everything was in place, nothing could go wrong. Before long I received a message.

Friend
Right, you ready?

Maxine
Yes, where shall I meet you?

Friend
I'll drive out the school gate and pull up on the left.

Maxine
OK, be 5 mins x

It was quiet at that time, mainly cleaners working their way through the building. I made my way towards Miss Lancashire's car. We were both very aware of our surroundings. There were no other cars in the car park and so it felt safe to meet her just outside of school. Once we drove out of familiar places, we both felt like we could relax. It had been a tough few months, so much had happened in such a short space of time, but I knew how I felt and I was happy to be around her. I felt I had grown up a lot. I was always broad minded but I started looking at life differently.

The drive up to Halifax took over two hours and when we got to the hotel, we were both ready to freshen up. It had been a long day. Miss Lancashire pulled into the huge car park, we got our bags out of the boot and headed for the reception. I remember looking around in awe. It was visually beautiful, a large grand building stood in the centre of the most stunning landscape. The building was surrounded by trees, plants and wild flowers. I had never seen anything like it. When we got to the reception desk, a nice young girl checked us in, and a hotel porter took our cases ready to show us to our room. Inside was just as beautiful as outside, tall ceilings, chandeliers. I remember feeling out of place but it suited Miss Lancashire so much.

We were only on the first floor when the hotel porter stopped us in the corridor.

"Okay, so we have put you in rooms next to each other, so which would you like Madam? 101 or 102?" I stared at him puzzled and then looked over to Miss Lancashire, who avoided eye contact with me.

"You got us separate rooms?" She took the keys from the hotel porter who looked very baffled.

"Thanks love, we can sort it now." The polite man walked away and Miss Lancashire turned to me.

"I will see you downstairs Maxine." She handed me a key and walked into her own room. I was so angry with her. She treated me like a child that she could do what she wanted with and I was sick of it. I let myself into my room and could not even appreciate how grand it was because of how rubbish I felt. I just wanted to go home. I noticed some flowers and chocolates she had arranged for me on the dressing table. I just did not understand why she did not want us to be together.

I decided to do what she had said. I got changed into my jumpsuit and re-applied my make-up. I took my hair down and curled it. Once I was ready, I made my way downstairs to the hotel bar. I saw Miss Lancashire sat in a corner near a fireplace. She had also changed into some black pants, a floral blouse, heeled boots, all topped off with a pearl necklace and matching earrings. Miss Lancashire always looked so elegant and classy. But I was mad. I approached her table and sat down.

"You look beautiful." she said.

"You are unbelievable."

"Maxine, what you have to remember…"

"I was so excited when you told me about this place and then you go and book separate rooms? I get it at school, but I am not fifteen any more, no one knows us here."

"This is not easy for me. I was going to book a double room, but I rang up and the words wouldn't come out."

"Why not? People can be gay, you know. The people who run the hotel don't care."

"Maxine…"

"What? It's what we are, isn't it? I mean, we're two women and we kiss, we have sex." I was agitated, getting more worked up. If I could come to terms with that, why couldn't she.

"Why are you acting like..." She trailed off.

"What?"

"Nothing."

"No, go on, like a child?" I snapped. It didn't matter how grown up I acted or looked; she still saw me as a child. Which I know you might be thinking I was. But it wasn't about age, it was about having respect for each other and trusting what we were doing. If she didn't trust me, then what was the point?

"We can still stay in the same room. I'm sorry. I am still getting used to this."

"No." I snapped. She'd made me so angry that I wasn't going to compromise like that. Miss Lancashire moved closer towards me.

"Sometimes I look at you and see this beautiful young lady, her whole life ahead of her – someone bright and kind, someone I want to be with. And then sometimes I see this young girl in her school uniform. I get overwhelmed. Let's not ruin this weekend." She took my hand over the table.

"Come on Maxine." She was desperate to get me back on side. I had a choice to make. I could carry on being mad with her or try and have a nice time. I decided to try.

After dinner we made our way upstairs. I went to walk into my room, but she put her arms around my waist.

"Come to my room." she said kissing me on my neck. I told her I was tired, so much had happened that day, yet again.

"Come to my room." she insisted and this time, I gave in. It was what I wanted, deep down, even if I was still feeling a bit frustrated by the whole thing. Miss Lancashire led the way. She put some music on the large TV and walked over to me. She kissed me softly, then more urgently, as she slowly started to undress me.

I woke up the next day, the sun beaming through the window onto my face. I looked over my shoulder, Miss Lancashire was asleep next to me. She was so beautiful. I remember looking around and feeling content. I also remember thinking about my parents and how they would feel if they could see me there in that hotel room with her. My eyes started to water when I thought about how much I had lied to them to keep it a secret. How much I loved them and how much I wanted to share this with them but I couldn't. Before I could think any more, Miss Lancashire started to wake up.

"Morning beautiful."
"Morning."
"You alright love?"
"I just can't believe we're here together". Miss Lancashire put her arm around me and pulled me into her. I closed my eyes feeling the safest I had ever felt. I asked myself as I held on to her, what defines a regret?

Can you regret something that's shaped you as a person but effectively changed your entire life? It's become so easy for people to have an opinion, to judge each other. It's so easy when you're on the other side looking in, to think you understand a situation. But in reality, no one knows how it feels, unless you have walked in that person's shoes. People say you get wiser as you get older. I don't think anyone gets wiser, not really. We are all just living and learning and we will keep making choices that people around us won't like or understand. But you just need to do what's right for you, live for today because no one knows how to make you happy, more than yourself.

Chapter 16
Close Call

Time was going so fast. The more time went on, the more normal it felt. Christmas was around the corner and it had been nearly six months since Miss Lancashire and I had started a relationship together. It had gone past the point of just fun, gone past the point of just something that was happening. It was starting to get serious. We knew each other as people outside of school. We had built a genuine relationship together. If we saw each other in the corridors at school or in assemblies, we would go out of our way to speak to each other. We couldn't help it, we wanted to be around each other. Education was always so important to me; my career plan was always so clear in my head. But I had new priorities and I didn't know what to do. I had a free period one afternoon and I went to see Miss Lancashire in her office.

"You alright love?"

"Yeah."

"Talk to me Maxine." I leaned forward on the chair.

"I have been thinking about after my A-levels."

"When you go to university?" Miss Lancashire looked at me over her glasses. I could tell she was already disapproving of what I was going to say.

"What if I didn't go?" I quickly said brushing past the subject.

"I beg your pardon?"

"What if I looked for a job in fashion straight away? You know, there are some good placements about."

"No Maxine, you are going to university. I told you when we started this, I will not get in the way of your studies."

"I don't want to move away."

"Why?"

"It's silly."

"Go on."

"I'm scared."

"Of what?"

"Losing you." Miss Lancashire moved closer to me, sitting on the chair next to mine. She gently moved my hair from my face.

"Don't be scared, I'm not going anywhere. But you are going to do amazing things and you won't do them here." She kissed me on the forehead and as she pulled away, we hovered close to each other. She leaned in and kissed me, it started slow, very slow where every sound could be heard. She held my face and I slowly leaned back into the chair. She unbuttoned my top and started touching my breasts. I had my hand under her blouse and was unfastening her bra. We were both lost in the moment. It shouldn't have happened, but it did, right there in her office. We got totally carried away.

"What's that?" Miss Lancashire pulled away from me. I could hear footsteps. Miss Lancashire put her hand over my mouth to be quiet. The footsteps got louder. They were getting closer to her office.

"Shit! Get your things, hide under here. Now Maxine!" Miss Lancashire rushed around her office fixing her clothes. I hid under her desk like she told me to. Miss

Lancashire sat down and tidied herself up. One knock at the door and it opened.

"Hello, some students are fighting in the English block, would you?"

"Brilliant, just what I need." Miss Lancashire followed the teacher out. I don't know who it was. I sighed with relief when they left. I waited until it felt safe and got up from under the desk. I left her office and headed for the A-level department in a panic. I sat in the canteen with a coffee and couldn't help but smile to myself. Even though what had just happened was scary and I could still feel my heart beating fast with adrenaline, I felt like the happiest girl in the world.

Chapter 17
Christmas

My family always made a big effort at Christmas. The house was decorated top to bottom with lights, tinsel, Christmas trees – all done very tastefully. Mum was very proud of her Christmas decorations. She always planned every detail, had a colour scheme and everything had it's place. That year was red and blue with white snow dotted around the house. Our Christmas tree was white and looked magical in the middle of the window, looking out onto the front garden. The red handmade baubles looked effortless on the branches, and a crystal star sat neatly at the top.

The build up to Christmas that year was special. It was the last Christmas that I remember with fond memories of my family. I always took family Christmas for granted and that year was no different, but we did have a good one. Everything was going so well at that time- I had settled into my A-levels, Lauren, Darcy and I were making more effort to meet up and stay in touch, and my relationship with Miss Lancashire was stronger than ever.

"Merry Christmas girlies." Chloe and I ran into the living room with excitement. Mum and Dad were snuggled by the fireplace waiting for us. Presents were piled under the tree, stockings hanging from the mantelpiece were filled with chocolates and sweets, and Christmas music was playing in the background. Chloe and I loved

Christmas, we loved it more the older we got. It was just as magical. And even though none of us believed in Santa anymore, we used to leave a mince pie, carrot and some milk out the night before that Dad would eat.

We always used to open our presents whilst we ate our breakfast, Mum's famous bacon butties. And then we would get dressed and wait for the family to arrive. The grandparents and aunties and uncles. We always had a big family affair. I got a laptop that year, and lots of designer clothing. My favourite was a pink *Chanel* bag which I had told Mum that I had liked ages before. Chloe got a bike and a new phone. We were always spoiled at Christmas, to us it was just normal because we always got a lot, but we still appreciated all our gifts.

"You seeing any young lad then love?" Grandad would say across the room, whilst sat in Dad's armchair, drinking a sherry. All the family would look to see my response. I would shake my head every time but this time I wanted to shout,

"Yes, actually I am seeing someone and I have been for ages! And she's amazing and it's going really well." But of course, I couldn't. My grandparents were very old-fashioned. I overheard conversations they would say about same sex couples on TV and it was not always pleasant. I worried about how they would react when they found out. I worried about everyone's reactions.

I didn't get to see Miss Lancashire that Christmas with all my family staying over. It was impossible to get away. We did message and have a brief chat over the phone but I felt sorry for her. Miss Lancashire did not have a strong relationship with her parents, she was an only child and never mentioned any aunties and uncles. She told me she went to see her parents that morning to have a coffee and exchange gifts but it was brief. Miss Lancashire spent Christmas with some of her close friends and their families. We would have liked to have seen each other with it being our first Christmas together. But I was happy she was not alone and she loved that I had a strong family network around me.

"Thank you." I walked into the conservatory that night. Mum and Dad were sharing a bottle of wine. Grandma and Grandad had gone back to their house and my aunties and uncles were in the living room playing some adult card games. I could hear my Auntie Steph bawling at something inappropriate my Uncle Bill had read out. Chloe was in her bedroom, watching a film.

"Come here." Mum opened her arms to me. I went and joined Mum and Dad on the sofa. Mum wrapped her arms around me like I was a baby, cradling me to sleep. In that moment it hit me. I was no longer a baby, no longer a little girl. I was an adult doing adult things. I squeezed my mum tight.

"I love you both, you know that don't you?"

"Of course we do, we love you too."

"Night." I went and sat on the stairs and watched through the slightly open door at my family having the best time. Mum and Dad joined them moments later, they were all laughing and joking, hugging each other, reminiscing about life. I walked upstairs and got into bed. I stared at the ceiling listening to my family until I fell asleep. Whatever was going to happen, my family would always have those memories to look back on. A day full of laughter and love.

Chapter 18
New Friends

    Going back to school after an exciting Christmas was alarming for me. I still had over one year to go at A-level. But I had teachers talking to me about mock exams for my modules and asking about my university choices. They were telling me I should really start thinking about my applications. Thinking about the things that used to excite me, now absolutely terrified me. I was always so sure of myself and my future but after everything that had happened, life just became more complicated. I told Miss Lancashire I was still going to go to university but only because she wouldn't let me say anything else. Every time I tried to speak to her about it, she would give me that look and would hear no more about it. The truth is I did want everything that I had always aspired to and worked hard for, but I did not want to leave her.

    A few weeks after the Christmas break, I was in art class when Miss Lyons introduced a new student to us, Tom Smith. He was from another *Sixth Form* college and came over to us just for the art module. He was very quirky looking, curly dark hair, baggy clothing, bright trainers. He looked confident and had a smile that would light up any room. His work station was next to mine so we got chatting and found we had a lot in common. We both loved fashion and wanted to study at the same university in London. We also found out we lived close by;

Tom lived just around the corner from me. He was a nice guy and I loved his passion for the subject. He became my A-level buddy. We did a lot of studying together and over time became close friends. One day during our art class, Tom looked over to me.

"So, there is this new restaurant in town, you fancy it?"

"Sounds nice, when are you thinking?"

"How about tonight?"

"Sure." I felt him smile and I could not help but smile back. I messaged Mum to let her know I would be home late. She was fine about it. After class, Tom and I were walking down the corridor together to leave school.

"Maxine." I heard from behind us. Miss Lancashire was stood further down the corridor.

"Can I have a word in my office please?" I told Tom to wait outside for me and I followed her to her office.

"Do you fancy doing something later?"

"Oh, I can't tonight. I'm having dinner with Tom. That's okay, isn't it? He's a good friend."

"Yes, of course it is. Have fun." Miss Lancashire kissed me on the cheek and then ushered me out of her office.

I went to meet Tom and we had a great night. We ate in a place called the *Dog and Bone* in the city centre – it was more of a pub but they did a fabulous pasta dish. He paid for everything and then he walked me home. Mum and Dad were in the garden when I got back, so they spotted him. They were polite, chatting for a bit before Tom left to go home. Mum gave me the look, smirking at me.

"No Mum." I said.

"He's cute." I heard mum shout after me.

It was nice having Tom in class, someone to enjoy the lessons with. I looked forward to seeing him at school and I think he looked forward to seeing me. Tom wasn't like the other boys I had come across. He was mature, passionate and so certain of himself. He knew what he wanted out of life and I admired his confidence. I have fond memories of Tom, but he became just another part of my situation and in the end I don't think he liked me very much. I guess he felt used. I don't blame him. I would have felt the same.

It was around February time and coming up to Miss Lancashire's birthday. I knew how old she was going to be but she hated taking about her age around me so we never discussed it. I think she felt paranoid but it didn't bother me. Miss Lancashire had booked the same apartment where we had gone for my sixteenth birthday. I could not wait to see it again, to make more memories together.

You might be thinking by now, how did we get away with it for so long? You might be thinking about my parents and asking where they thought I was? But it became so normal. Just routine. It was the same old sleepover lie, staying late at school. I would make up new friends at school that my parents were desperate to meet but did not exist. I guess I became good at lying. I wasn't a bad teenager and so they believed me. I was doing well at school and they gave me the freedom I always wanted. They trusted me.

That night, Miss Lancashire and I laid in bed watching rubbish TV and casually chatting. Later on in the evening I gave her my present which was a drawing of us in a frame that I had done. I made her a card too. She loved those gifts and almost cried when she saw the picture I had drawn.

"Where do you live?" I asked her.

"I have a house down Chance Avenue."

"Can I come over one day?"

"Would you like that?" I nodded.

"Of course you can then." I leaned into her.

"Can we get some wine?" I said with a huge smile on my face. Miss Lancashire put her arms around me.

"You my love are underage. I cannot possibly allow you to drink." We both laughed. Miss Lancashire got out of bed and pulled a bottle of red out of her bag.

"Will this do?" I smiled and watched her pour it for us. Miss Lancashire passed me a glass and sat at the end of the bed. It went silent for a while.

"So. Tom. Did you have a nice afternoon the other day?"

"Oh, the meal? Yeah, it was nice."

"You never mentioned it, that's all."

"There was nothing to mention, we are friends."

"That's good, it's good to have friends."

"You said it was okay."

"Yes it is, of course it is, you can have friends Maxine." The mood changed instantly. She drank from her glass. I took a drink from mine too, avoiding eye contact.

"I'm tired Maxine, we should sleep."

"Okay." Miss Lancashire finished her wine and took mine off me before I had chance to finish it. She turned off the lights and we got into bed. She did not say another word to me until the next day. When we woke up, she was fine with me. All was back to normal, but I still felt like there was something on her mind. Something she wanted to say but was holding back. I decided not to ask.

Chapter 19
Paranoia

As time went on Miss Lancashire began to message me all the time, even during class time. My phone was going off so much, I started turning it off. One afternoon I saw Miss Lancashire in the car park, taking boxes out of her car. I decided enough was enough.
"What's going on?"
"You're alive then." Her tone was cold.
"What are you talking about?"
"You never answer your phone."
"I'm busy, I'm doing my A-levels Miss. My A-levels. I thought you wanted me to do well?"
"And when you're at home? Or are you with Tom?"
"Do you know how stupid that makes you sound!" I said walking away from her. I was agitated and annoyed.
"Maxine, do not walk away from me." I didn't listen. I didn't look back. I kept walking until I got to the Sixth Form canteen. I had never spoken to Miss Lancashire like that before, but actually, it felt quite refreshing at the time. I had not been in a situation like that before, so it was all new to me. I just had to react in the moment as things were happening. That's all I could honestly do.

Miss Lancashire came looking for me that day, she followed me into the study room. She apologised and said that she would make it up to me. The messages were less intense, and we seemed to be back to normal. Whatever normal was now. Miss Lancashire and I were in a good place, but so were me and Tom.

    I was in English one Friday when someone knocked on the door. It was Miss Smith from reception. She had some roses in her hand. Everyone laughed because it was a very odd situation. She said that they were for me. I went red and I could hear the class muttering to each other. Mrs Finn handed them to me. I read the card and it said *Tom x*. It was very sweet and word soon got around the *Sixth Form*. I could feel the other students staring at me when I walked into the canteen and study room. He asked me if I could meet him after school in the art room. I did what he wanted and when I got there he was sat with some chocolates. I felt this overwhelming sensation throughout my body. There was no stopping this guy.

    "I know this might be geeky – the flowers and everything – but I really like you, and this is where we met so I thought we could just, ya know." I laughed and went to sit down. We had a laugh like always, it was like out of a film. I did not know guys did things like that, they probably didn't. Tom was one of a kind. We only stayed at school for half an hour because Miss Lyons made a joke about wanting her classroom back. So Tom walked me home.

    After the stressful situation I had going on with Miss Lancashire, my friendship with Tom seemed like a breath of fresh air. I felt relaxed when I was with him and I really enjoyed his company. He turned to me at the bottom of my drive and out of nowhere, he kissed me on the lips. It all happened so fast before I could react. He smiled nervously.

"I'm sorry, that was..." I stood there trying not to come across as awkward.

"No, it's okay." The only thing in my head when I said that was Miss Lancashire.

"Thanks Tom, for today, see you soon." I smiled at him as he walked back down the road. It was only a kiss; it did not mean anything. Who was I kidding? Tom liked me, and I was giving him no indication that I was not interested. What a mess.

I remember the weekend after the kiss. I was texting Tom probably more than Miss Lancashire. I remember Miss Lancashire getting snappy with me over message. It was late one Saturday night when she said to me that she was really busy and would see me next week. So I stopped messaging her and messaged Tom instead. It was just casual messages, maybe it was flirty at times but we were just having fun.

"So, you going to let me take you out again tomorrow?" Tom said during art class. He tried to be discreet but our classmates heard and Miss Lyons came over.

"You okay Tom?" he nodded and I smirked at Miss Lyons who smiled back whilst shaking her head.

"Time and a place Tom, time and a place." she said before moving around the classroom.

"I will need to check my diary." I said whispering. We didn't have to be in silence in art but I absolutely did not want everyone knowing our conversations, especially after the flowers. People were already talking and I did not want it to get back to Miss Lancashire.

I did end up meeting him the next day in town. We met outside the shopping centre. He clearly made an effort with his outfit; he wore black slim cut trousers and a nice blue shirt. He'd gone a bit heavy on the Lynx too. I could smell him before I could see him. We went to the cinema to watch a film. I don't remember the name but it had a lot of car chase scenes in it, lots of explosions. Not my cup of tea but there weren't many choices and I didn't mind.

I remember halfway through the film realising where I was and feeling a sense of guilt take over my body. Tom was a good friend but I was leading him on. He tried to hold my hand a few times and touch my leg. I moved away and I could sense that he was confused. After the film he took me for dinner and bowling. He tried hugging me towards the end of the evening but I pulled away once more. I couldn't do it; it did not feel right.

"You okay?" Tom asked.

"I think I want to go home, thanks Tom." I said walking away from the bowling alley.

"Maxine, what's going on?" I felt horrible not looking back but I couldn't without wanting to cry. Why did I feel like I was cheating? Nothing really happened with Tom, apart from the kiss but that was nothing – well, for me anyway.

When I got in that night, I messaged Miss Lancashire telling her I had spent the day with Tom and that I missed her. She never replied.

It soon became very awkward at school. You would think because Miss Lancashire was the head teacher, I could avoid her. She spent most of her time in her office. But in fact, it was worse because she could always get hold of me if she wanted. I was expecting Miss Lancashire to take me to one side and talk to me about spending the day with Tom, but she never did. I bumped into her talking to another student at school but she just blanked me. I knew she wasn't happy with me but she wouldn't even text me back and was clearly avoiding me. I didn't know what to do. I kept thinking about what I should say to her. Do I tell her the truth about the kiss? Or just miss that bit out? I didn't want to lie to her but I didn't want to make her angry either. So I didn't do anything. I waited and waited until it got worse, and eventually it did.

  The week after, Tom came into art class looking a little upset. I asked him if he was okay and he just smiled and nodded. He was quiet, there was something very different about him. That smile he had was no longer genuine. I thought maybe he had realised that I was not interested in that way. I still wanted to be his friend though, I cared for him. I tried to engage more with him but he never seemed to be fully there, his mind was always wondering. It was like he was avoiding me. I didn't blame him for being angry with me. I was sending him mixed emotions. I should have just been straight with him. I hoped we could at least be civil in class though. I managed to corner him one afternoon in the canteen.
  "What's going on?" I asked him.
  "Nothing, it's okay, I get it now."
  "Get what?"
  "Miss Lancashire's told me." I paused for a moment realising what Tom had said. Why would she do that? It's not like what we are doing was all above board.
  "What do you mean?"

"That you already have a boyfriend outside school." Miss Lancashire did not tell him the truth about us. She lied to him and I didn't understand why she would go out of her way to ruin my friendship with Tom. The worst part was, I now had to lie to him again and pretend that what she had said was true. I was devastated that Tom would think I was some horrible little cheat.

"Tom, I'm sorry. I wanted to tell you but..."

"No worries." Tom walked away from me deflated, like he couldn't be bothered any more. He really did make an effort with me and I felt like I destroyed his spirit. What kind of person was I turning into? I was angry and upset. I wanted answers, so I ran to Miss Lancashire's office and let myself in.

"Why would you..." Before I could finish, I stopped myself. Miss Lancashire was sat with Mr Watson going over some paperwork. I could see he was confused and Miss Lancashire looked like she could have killed me. I froze. I didn't know what to do. Miss Lancashire stood up.

"How dare you barge in here. What is it Maxine?"

"Sorry Miss, I thought someone else was in here with you. Sorry." I left as quickly as I could feeling terrible. All I wanted to do was ring Lauren and Darcy and talk to them but I couldn't. I was alone.

I went and sat in the study room. I liked it in there, it was quiet. I used to watch the other students getting on with their work. I would watch teachers come and go to help them. In my head I would tell them what was happening, hoping for some ideas on how to deal with it better, ideas on what to do. It helped a little bit but not much. When Miss Lancashire and I were good, it was the best feeling ever. But when we were bad it was the worst.

About an hour later, I got a message from Miss Lancashire.

Friend
My car. After school. 4.30. Usual place. No questions.

Now I was in trouble again. Sometimes I did not know how I had got to that point. My once stress-free life, with nothing but good grades and my looks to worry about, was now absolute chaos. I did what she asked because I just wanted to get it over with. I went to the bottom of my road and got in her car. Miss Lancashire did not look at me, she just drove. It was silent for a while.
"Anything you want to tell me?" she finally said. I shook my head staring at the window at the people living their normal lives.
"You know Maxine, we have been doing this – whatever this is – for a long time now. And I did not think you would lie to me." I did not say anything. I just sat awkward wanting to be saved from the situation.
"I know you know I had a chat with Tom. Just to make sure he was not distracting you. I mean, flowers being delivered? We're a school, not a florist. It was very interesting. I knew he liked you. It was written all over his face. I asked him if you two were a thing, he smiled and wouldn't say anything, but I knew. You kissed him, didn't you?"
I paused thinking about how to tell her and then like an idiot I said,
"No."
"Do not lie to me!" I could see how angry she was getting. Eventually I told her the truth.

"Yes, but..." Miss Lancashire snapped. She put her foot down, the car was going too fast for the road we were on. I started to panic. I wanted her to stop. I wanted to go home.

"Miss please! You're scaring me." She was unstoppable, she went crazy. I had never seen anything like that before. She had lost control.

Chapter 20
Love Conquers

    Miss Lancashire braked suddenly which made us both jolt forward. She hit the steering wheel with her hand, before hitting her head hard on the wheel. She was muttering to herself. I knew she was not going to be pleased but I never expected her to react like that. She was acting insane.
    "Get out."
    "What? Why?" I started to feel scared. Miss Lancashire got out the car, opened my side of the door and dragged me out the car.
    "Get out Maxine!" She threw me on the muddy grass. I fell on my front and could do nothing but cry. I did not deserve this, did I? Was I that bad a person?
    "Now you think about what it is you really want Maxine, because I cannot do this. I am risking everything for you." Miss Lancashire got back in her car and drove off. I shouted at her to come back, crying on the floor, but she did not stop. I was in a cold, muddy field. My phone had no signal and it was not like I could just ring my parents. I mean, what could I say to them? I threw myself back on the grass and closed my eyes, hoping to wake up back when I was fifteen, a couple of weeks before my exams.

For the first time I think it hit me. What I was doing. What I had been doing for so long. Being on top of that hill was one of the worst things that ever happened to me. But it came to be one of the best. It gave me time to work things out and put my life into perspective. When I imagined a life without Miss Lancashire, I couldn't do it. I never thought about been gay when I was younger. I knew of it but it never occurred to me that I might be. I always liked guys, had crushes on guys from the TV. But I did like her, and I never felt anything when Tom kissed me, so maybe I was gay. Maybe this was who I had been all along.

I then started thinking about the age gap and the fact that she was a teacher, not only that but she was the head teacher. I kept thinking that once I was at university, it would not be that bad. Maybe when I got to a certain age, people would not even care. Lauren and Darcy might judge me at first but then I thought they would come around because we were meant to be best friends. Then there was my family. I knew they would not be happy. They would be disappointed in me but I was sure in time they could get past it. I could not even think how I would tell them. But after thinking about all of that, it seemed like nothing compared to how I would feel if I never saw Miss Lancashire again.

It seemed like ages up on that hill, alone. I thought about walking to try and find someone, but I had seen films and heard stories about young girl's going missing. So I decided to stay put. Time went past. I became tired, restless, worried that she would not come back for me. I looked at my phone with 51% battery and no signal. My parents were going to be so worried. Yet again I was putting them through something horrible. I tried to ring and text Miss Lancashire to come back, but nothing was going through.

After a while, I saw car lights in the distance. The car stopped. Miss Lancashire got out of the car. She stood for a while just staring at me. She looked a mess; all her make-up was smudged and her hair looked like she'd being running her hands through it with stress. A few moments passed and finally she opened her arms to me. I got up from the grass and ran to her sobbing. I must have needed to breakdown because I did, good and proper. She held me so tight.

"It's okay, I've got you, I am so sorry." In that moment I knew. I just knew what I had to do. She drove me home that night and just before I got out, she looked over to me.

"Maxine… I love you." Only my family had ever said that to me before and Lauren and Darcy but they were practically family. It made my tummy flutter inside. I smiled and got out the car. I was emotionally and physically exhausted.

Things started to get more serious after the night on the hill. I started to deteriorate in regards to my studies. I wanted to do well, but I could feel myself losing motivation. I would often skip lessons to avoid being in confrontation with Tom. It was hard seeing him. I know we were young and that he would get over it, but I think he felt embarrassed more than anything. My parents started to notice a difference in me too. They were asking questions about Tom and I, giving me advice on relationships. If only they knew. I did my best to get things done at home for my studies, but I was receiving letters of concern every other week from my teachers. Miss Lancashire was on at me to make sure I finished my A-levels and that she could not be the reason I failed them. Things were just harder; it became harder to hide. I decided I no longer wanted to live a lie. I was so fed up.

Chapter 21
Home Truths

    My education always meant so much to me and yet I found myself struggling to find any motivation for studying. I was losing commitment. Summer was not too far away. Time was going so fast and it scared me because I was not ready to leave what I had with Miss Lancashire behind. I tried to focus, I really did, but I couldn't. Perhaps I had a new passion, a new direction I wanted to take my life in. I knew I always wanted to finish my A-levels and go on to university, and that's what my parents and Miss Lancashire wanted for me too. But I wasn't feeling it any more. The hardest part was not being able to tell my family, not been able to confide in my mum.

    I started to watch my family all the time, taking in every detail. I would watch them at dinner times, movie nights, when we would go out for meals. I tried to give them good times, make them smile, make them laugh, tell them how much I loved them. I wanted them to have good memories because I knew one day how much I was going to break their hearts.

    I messaged Miss Lancashire one evening asking if we could meet. She was the only one that I could talk to about everything. She invited me around to her house. I was shocked because she always used to put it off. I had wanted to go to hers for so long and I felt like we were taking another big step forward. I couldn't wait. Miss

Lancashire's house was really overwhelming. It was a modern, three-bed detached house in a posh area of Manchester, the front drive was huge. It was very luxurious inside, furnished to perfection, there was nothing out of place. Everything was colour-coordinated, silver and grey. The lavender smell was strong just like in her office. When I arrived, she was so welcoming. I was nervous stepping over her threshold.

"Can I get you a drink love?"

"Yes please."

"Wine or Juice?"

"Wine please." I had started to get used to the taste of wine and I loved drinking with her. Miss Lancashire took my coat and I followed her into the living room. She ushered me to sit down and then left to the kitchen. I remember thinking at the time how amazing it must feel to have achieved so much in your life like she had. To live in such a beautiful house that you have worked so hard for. I wanted that, even more so after seeing hers.

"Here you go darling." Miss Lancashire passed me a glass of red wine.

"Thank you. Your house is amazing."

"Bless you. I do love this house. So everything okay with you?"

"I am really trying with school but I'm struggling."

"Yes I know, nearly all of your subject teachers have expressed concern to me. I should have sent a letter to your parents weeks ago but I know you can pull this around. I've been slipping too. I've missed a few meetings myself with one thing and another. Right pair, aren't we?"

"Do you think this will ever be normal?"

"I don't know love. It's complicated."

"Yeah, I know. I hate lying to everyone, my mum. I feel like I've lost everyone." Miss Lancashire moved to sit next to me on the sofa, she put her arm around me.

"We will get through this Maxine. I will make sure you get through this." I nodded feeling more reassured.

"Right, shall we order some pizza? I'm starving." I nodded.

"Can I use your bathroom?"

"Yes of course – upstairs, first door on the left."

I knew that whatever was going to happen from that point would not be easy. But nothing could prepare me for what was about to happen next. Nothing at all.

Miss Lancashire's house was massive and I could not help myself, my eyes were wondering everywhere. After I had left the bathroom, I started to look around. The landing area was a big rectangle with four doors at the top. The large staircase was in the centre going downstairs. There was a glass cabinet to the right with pictures in. I looked closely at the pictures. They were of Miss Lancashire and her family – on holiday, when she graduated, when she was young. She really was so beautiful, really long blond hair and tanned skin. I should have stopped there and gone back downstairs. But when I stood at the top of the stairs, one of the doors caught my eye. It had a pink crown on it. I stood, contemplating what to do. I could hear Miss Lancashire on the phone to the takeaway so I decided to go and have a look.

I walked to the door, the crown on the door had been painted on. I opened the door slightly and carefully walked in trying not to make a sound. I could not believe my eyes. It was a young girl's bedroom. There was a single bed in the middle under the window, pink curtains draped over it. I remember the pink dressing table to the left and the room was full of teddies and doll-houses. There was a picture on the bedside table. I went over to it. I stood for a few seconds staring at the picture.

"What are you doing?" Miss Lancashire was stood in the door way.

"You know it's rude to go snooping Maxine."

"Who's this?" I asked very confused. I pointed to the picture of Miss Lancashire hugging a young blonde girl. They were on holiday. Miss Lancashire took the picture and held my hand to sit down on the bed. She looked tense.

"Maxine, there is something I have not told you." My hands went clammy. I felt myself start to shake with worry.

"Just tell me." I pleaded.

"Her name is Hannah." She paused for some time.

"She is my daughter."

I could not believe what she was saying to me.

"But, how?" I started to get upset not understanding fully.

"My first relationship. I was with a guy called William. I met him at university, he was studying to be a teacher too. It wasn't planned, we were drunk. I found out I was pregnant four months in." I pulled my hand away from hers.

"How could you not tell me this? I'm done with you." I got up to leave. Miss Lancashire grabbed hold of my arms.

"Maxine, no!"

"We cannot possibly carry on now, look at her!" I took the picture from her.

"You have a daughter."

"Maxine, please listen to me." It got heated as we both shouted over each other. Well, I shouted and she tried to calm me down. I ran down the stairs and got my bag. I headed to the door but she got in front of me.

"This photo was taken a long time ago."

"Will you open the door please?"

"Listen to me, you stupid little girl...she's dead!"

Silence.

Miss Lancashire walked into the kitchen. I froze. I had so many questions, and needed so many answers. After a few moments, I followed her.

"Dead? I don't understand." Miss Lancashire poured herself some wine and drank it in one mouthful, she filled the glass again.

"She died on a skiing holiday, she was only ten, she had her whole life ahead of her and was taken in an instant. I had a breakdown. William and I became like strangers, we were not compatible anymore. The pressures exposed deep flaws in our relationship and so one day I just got up and left. I needed a fresh start. It's not something you just tell someone Maxine. I didn't plan to tell you like this." Miss Lancashire crumbled. I took a moment and went over to her. I took hold of her hands.

"I'm sorry."

"Please Maxine, this can't change anything between us, you have given me so much, more than you will ever know. You have given me my life back."

"Do I remind you of her?"
"Hannah was the light bulb in my life. When she died, it went off. Then I met you, this fiery, sassy, intelligent, beautiful girl. I don't know if this is sounding weird. But you just gave me my light back." I stared at her, my eyes watering with sadness. Looking at a woman who had lost the most important thing in her life, her only child. I kissed her. I kissed her like I had never kissed her before. She kissed me back, our faces wet with tears. We were overemotional, overtired, confused, upset, so many feelings.

Miss Lancashire spent the whole of that night telling me about her daughter, Hannah.

"Hannah was so creative, she was always making and drawing things for me. She wanted to be an artist when she grew up, she used to get so giddy when she thought about all the jobs she could do for a living. For someone so young, she was very mature. She always wanted to better herself, she always wanted to achieve. I was so proud of her. We were all very excited to go on our first skiing holiday together. I went skiing a lot when I was a child and I couldn't wait to share my love for it with Hannah and William. I remember watching her from the bottom of the mountain. I had only just got off the cable cart. I could see her in her bright pink coat she used to love. She looked so tiny. I remember watching her. Something wasn't right. She was going too fast. I could see her losing control, she steered off into some nearby woods. I was screaming at William to go and help her. But he was so far away. She crashed into a tree and was knocked unconscious. Hannah never woke up. It should have been one of the best experiences of Hannah's life. But she never made it home."

For the first time since the accident, Miss Lancashire opened up to me and let her feelings be heard. Life was now becoming very real for both of us. I knew that one day very soon, I would need to make my bed and lie in it.

Chapter 22
Two Worlds Collide

It was a Thursday afternoon, summer was fast approaching and with it, my seventeenth birthday. In a way I could not wait to get older. I kept thinking if people were to find out when I was eighteen, then it would look less bad. You can do so much at eighteen, you're finally an adult. I just needed to be out of school and out of the student-teacher zone.

I was at school studying. I had a lot of free periods so it was a pretty relaxed day. I had a nice spot in the IT room, in the corner away from everyone working on the computers. I had all my books out, my laptop on the side, my music playing through my headphones. It was just what I needed. A good study day to try and get back into my work. I had been seeing Miss Lancashire for nearly a year by that point. Sometimes I used to think how on earth it had happened. It seemed so long ago since I had walked into Miss Lancashire's office on results day. So much had happened since that first kiss.

I was sat quietly when Tom came into the study room. I could see him walking in, but I did not look up straight away. Tom and I were okay by that point. We still enjoyed class together but that was it. We were friends and finally that was clear. I took my earphones out and was shocked to see how tired he looked.

"You okay?" I asked.

"I need to talk to you about something."

"Okay."

"I am only telling you this because I still care about you."

"Just say it Tom, it can't be that bad."

"There's a rumour going around."

"Okay."

"It's about you and Miss Lancashire." I felt my heart sink. I started to sweat.

"What?"

"I was in the canteen the other day, people were saying you two have been seen outside school together, someone said they saw you at the cinema". I felt sick. I knew that everything he was telling me was true but I couldn't tell him the truth.

"That is ridiculous, and none of it's true- obviously." I gathered my things together in a hurry. Tom did not know what to do. I could see him slowly get the courage to leave. At least when Lauren and Darcy were suspicious, I could control the situation. Now rumours were spreading and I had no idea where from.

I ran to Miss Lancashire's office. When I got there, she was not in. I started to panic and get worked up. Everyone that I saw- teachers and students, I felt like they knew. I couldn't breathe.

"Maxine." I turned round and Mrs Davis was stood in the corridor, she had clearly been looking for me.

"Can you come with me please?"

"I can't Miss, I need to..."

"Now." she insisted.

I followed Mrs Davis into her office. The walk was awful, she never spoke to me at all. In my head I was trying to work out what to say. What could I say to make this go away? And where the hell was Miss Lancashire? Mrs Davis held her office door open for me, she told me to sit down. I watched her close the door and sit down at her desk. Her office was much smaller than Miss Lancashire's, too small for the occasion. I felt trapped. Mrs Davis folded her arms on the desk, studying my body language.

"Now, I am going to ask you something Maxine, and I want you to know that you can tell me anything in the strictest confidence."

"Okay."

"Is there anything you want to tell me about Miss Lancashire?" I could feel my eyes start to water, but I could not let her see me break down, because I was scared that once I started, I would not be able to stop.

"I don't know what you mean."

"If she has acted inappropriate with you, you need to tell me."

"Inappropriate?"

"For example, you've never spent time with Miss Lancashire outside school? Gone to her office without needing to? Texting? Anything like that?"

"Miss Lancashire's been helping me with my workload and university applications, that's all. Sometimes I go to her office for her help." Mrs Davis stared at me with a look of concern. I couldn't tell if she was convinced or not.

"Okay, you know my door is always open."

"Please can I go?"

"Where are you going to go?"

"What?"

"When you leave my office, where is it you're going to go?"

"To the toilets and then to the study room." Mrs Davis sat back in her chair.

"You can go, but I am keeping my eye on you Maxine." I nodded.

I walked around school in a state, looking down every corridor, looking into every classroom. I could not see Miss Lancashire anywhere. I tried to call her, text her but she never replied. I cannot even imagine how much of a mess I must have looked. I heard the bell go for break and suddenly the corridor was swamped with students. In all the chaos and noise, I finally heard my phone buzz, it was a text.

Friend
Come to my office now!

I felt my heart race. I quickly made my way over. When I got there, she was already waiting for me. I rushed in.

"It's okay. I know." I could tell she was flustered.

"Where the hell have you been? I thought you left me." I started to cry; it was all getting too much.

"I would never leave you. Now we have to be smart, Maxine, this day was always going to come. I just wish it was later."

"How do you know?"

"I was having a drink with a friend last night, he told me of the rumours that were going around the staff at a rival high school nearby. I was going to message you but I did not want to worry you. I will sort it." I could not believe what was happening. I remember feeling overwhelmed with worry. We had come this far without been caught. How could another high school staff room be talking about us?

"I have just been with Mrs Davis; she's been asking me about you."

"What did you say?"

"Nothing, but she said she is going to be keeping her eye on me."

"Try to get through today Maxine. I need to sort some things out now and then I'm going to call at your house tonight."

"No Miss, please."

"I'm not going to say anything. Just act normal. You need to trust me, okay? Now you really need to go." Miss Lancashire hugged me and lead me out of her office. I made my way back to the study room and hid away in a corner. I couldn't wait for the bell to go to go home. I sat there for the next five hours, not moving a muscle. It was like the night on top of the hill again. The realisation of what we were doing. The fact that it was normal to us but to the rest of the world it would be anything but.

Once the after-school bell had gone, I quickly made my way home. Mum was already there preparing food for tea.

"You alright love?"

"Yeah fine." I took my shoes off and ran to the bathroom where I sobbed quietly until Mum shouted me down for tea. I took a breath before walking into the dining room. Dad was working late that night so we ate tea without him. I tried to act normal and engage in conversation but I had no energy. I felt exhausted with worry. I did not want to eat but luckily it was a soup, so I just soaked it in bread and left most of the bread. I wanted Miss Lancashire to text me so I knew what was going on. But she never replied to any of my messages.

Later on in the evening I was in my room, sat on my bed in the dark. I heard Dad come home, I heard him in the shower and then he went downstairs to warm his tea. Not long after, the doorbell went. I froze. My heart started racing. I made my way downstairs and sat at the dining table. I had never been so scared. Mum got up from the sofa, she was watching a film with Chloe, and answered the door.

"Hello, my name is Jane Lancashire. I am the head teacher at *Broadfield High School.* Please may I come in?" Chloe ran across to the window to look.

"Hi, yeah, come on in." Dad made his way to the hallway.

"Everything alright?" I heard Dad ask. Mum showed Miss Lancashire into the living room. I was still sat at the dining table. Chloe was still stood near the window. Miss Lancashire glanced at me. She was very professional and calm.

"Do you mind if we sit?"

"Yeah sure." Mum suggested Miss Lancashire sit at the dining table too, Dad followed.

"Chloe, why don't you go and run yourself a nice bath?" Mum said wanting to get her out the way. Chloe went upstairs reluctantly. I think she was worried about missing something. I could barely look at Miss Lancashire, but I could feel Mum and Dad looking at me, but I just stayed focused and did my best to act normal and not break down.

"First of all, I want to apologise for coming without warning. I'm not sure how to start this conversation. It's ludicrous but I am aware of some rumours going around the school. Rumours involving myself and Maxine." I was sweating wondering what on earth she was going to say next.

"People are saying that we are involved."

"Involved how?" Mum said.

"Sexually I'm afraid." Miss Lancashire said avoiding eye contact with me. I went red. I did not know what I should do. What did Miss Lancashire want me to do?

"Are you serious?" Dad's voice was quiet, ominous.

"You see Maxine and I have been spending a lot of time together in school. I have been helping her with her *UCAS* applications for university. I wanted to come to you in person before the rumours get out of hand. I am working with the school to make sure these rumours are addressed."

"You know what kids are like." I said with very little confidence.

"Thanks for letting us know." Dad got up and left the room. I heard him put the microwave on.

"Well thanks for coming." Mum got up too. She was polite but she was clearly concerned.

"Not at all. I am very sorry about this. Enjoy the rest of your night." Mum showed Miss Lancashire to the door. Mum came back into the living room, she sat on the sofa with her back to me and started reading a magazine.

"Mum." She did not answer me. I went upstairs and threw up in the toilet. I did not see Dad again for the rest of the night.

Later in the evening, I heard Mum and Dad arguing. I heard my name mentioned a lot. I wanted to go down to them but I couldn't. I was scared of what I might say. That night, it was around 1.00AM in the morning when I heard my bedroom door open- it was Mum. She came in and sat at the end of my bed.

"Maxine, there is no truth in these rumours are there?" I could see she was upset. I hated lying to her.

"No of course not." I said feeling disgusted that I could lie to her face so easily. But there was something in the way I looked at her and the way she looked at me after I said that. She would never admit it now. But my mum knew in that moment. She knew that it was all true. The words I used were lies but my eyes couldn't. She had probably known for a long time but would never say it out loud. Not until she had to. She gave me a hug, the last hug she would ever give me. I was texting Miss Lancashire all night asking what we should do.

After that night it was hard for me to focus on school. The rumours only got worse. I had people sniggering at me, calling me horrible names on social media. My family saw it all and it became harder for them to believe me. Too much was being said by all kinds of people in our area. There was no escaping it. My dad spoke to Lauren and Darcy who told them about my sixteenth birthday, results day and what they had seen and heard in the past. I could not believe they would betray me like that.

I only had nearly one year of my A-levels left and I could not even face going into school anymore. My teachers were even acting different with me. Miss

Lancashire was having her own difficulties trying to contain all the rumours. She was not in school much anymore. Mr Watson had taken over her main duties. I decided enough was enough. After that night everything happened so fast.

"I quit Miss. I quit." It was 3.00AM and I had snuck out to meet Miss Lancashire in the park opposite the school. Miss Lancashire started crying.
"Maxine, I am so sorry this has happened. I never wanted this for you."
"What do we do?"
"Listen to me, what happens now is not going to be nice for any of us. It's going to be hard and I am not sure what the outcome will be. But remember all the good, and whatever people say to you, I do care for you and I do love you." Miss Lancashire pulled me in for a hug. She was the only person in the entire world that understood how it felt. I felt like she was all I had.
I had only just snuck back in after meeting Miss Lancashire in the park, when I heard my bedroom door creek open. It was Chloe, she came and got into bed with me. I wrapped the quilt tightly around us both.
"You've been crying." Her voice was small. I did not answer.
"I know it's true, what they're all saying."
"No, it's not." I said exhausted.
"I always knew. I just didn't know she was a teacher."
"Chloe, what are you talking about?"

"I saw you in her car on your birthday. I was watching from the bathroom window. I saw you kiss." I could not believe what I was hearing.

"Chloe, I am so sorry." I started to sob. Chloe cuddled me.

"Just be happy, just be happy." Ten years old and she was the one cradling me to sleep telling me it was all going to be okay. For someone so young, she was very mature and I was proud of her, so proud of her.

Chapter 23
Brought Back To Reality

Everything started escalating pretty quickly at school. Miss Lancashire was still working as the head teacher but it wasn't easy for her. I was trying to get through my A-levels until summer, then I planned to never go back. It was hard because no one wanted to talk to me or work with me, even the teachers were being off with me, wary of how to treat me. They would either look at me with disgust or want to take me in their arms and offer support which I did not need. I was avoiding Mrs Davis too because I heard that she wanted to see me in her office and I could not be bothered with the confrontation. Mum and Dad had been brought into school too, and we all had to talk to the police. It was all getting very real and very messy. Everyone was confused because we were still both denying it and there wasn't any real evidence. The police were only involved because the teachers had expressed concern to Miss Lancashire and other higher members of staff. They could not ignore what they were hearing from the students. So Miss Lancashire had to get the police in herself. It was almost like a double bluff.

    The moment I decided I was done, was when I was in art class. Miss Lyons was talking to us about our projects but I wasn't listening. I was just staring out of the window, thinking about my school and home life. Trying to get to a point in my head where I was at some sort of peace. I looked to Miss Lyons who was still talking to the class. I stood up; Miss Lyons stopped talking.

"I'm done now Miss." I left the classroom with a sense of relief. Miss Lyons was shouting after me but I carried on and on, down the corridor and out the front door. I sat on the grass opposite the reception area at the front of the school. The sun was shining, such a peaceful day. I could see some classes taking place through the windows. The staff in reception getting on with their jobs, the PE class in the courts, everyone getting on with their life's oblivious to my current situation.

I sat on the grass and remembered all the good times I had. My first day, meeting my teachers for the first time, all those memories with Lauren and Darcy, school trips, GCSE results, meeting Miss Lancashire – my life flashed before my eyes. I put my head in my hands and just sobbed. I could feel the heat on my body from the sun. After a moment I felt someone touch my shoulder,

"Maxine, how did it get to this?" I looked up and it was Mrs Finn. She sat down beside me.

"Please tell me it's not true?" I did not answer but my reaction said it all.

"You have so much potential Maxine. I wish there was something I could say to stop whatever it is that's happening. Just please promise me something? Talk to someone, whoever it is, please don't be alone."

"I promise Mrs".

"Good luck Maxine." Mrs Finn left. I watched her walk back into school, she looked back and held her hand up to me. I smiled.

"Thank you." I whispered."Thank you."

I went home that night from school in a state of shock. When I got through the door Dad had packed a bag for me. I could hear Mum and Chloe crying upstairs. I felt my heart break at that moment. I could not even bring myself to say anything. I just smiled politely, picked up the bag and left. My dad was crying, I was crying. I decided not to call Miss Lancashire straight away. I went and sat in the local park. It was only a ten minute walk from home. It was still light out. I sat on a bench near the play area wondering where it all went wrong.

Out of nowhere, a small poodle came running towards me, fussing around my feet. I went to stroke it.

"Sorry! Benji, come on, that's..." a voice said from the distance. I looked up and it was her, it was Lucy Blackmore.

"Maxine Watts." Lucy was as shocked as I was. She stood hands on hips, shaking her head in disbelief. I hadn't seen Lucy since results day – she hadn't changed much; she was still half dressed and scruffy. Her hair was longer now, she had dyed it dark red, it was in a long pony tail. She was bigger than she was at school. She picked up her dog and started walking away.

"Lucy, don't go." I said, a little desperate. I moved my bag for her to sit next to me. She paused for a moment and then walked over to me. None of us said anything for a while.

"I'm not fat by the way, I'm pregnant." she blurted out. That's the Lucy I remembered; bold and in your face.

"So you can take that gossip to all of your popular mates and bitch about me."

"I'm not going to bitch about you Lucy. Congratulations." Lucy looked at me shocked that I had said something nice.

"So, what you up to? You will be going to uni soon? Moving away from here- you- with your perfect life." I did not want to tell Lucy what was going on. I didn't even know if I liked her.

"My life's not perfect."

"I bet you're looking at me thinking I turned out how you imagined, up the duff, no job, no money."

"Do you have family around you?"

"Yeah, I have my mum."

"Then you're not doing so bad." The poodle started yapping a little way off from us.

"Aww Benji." Lucy got up to chase him off some other dog's toy.

"Laters Maxine."

"Lucy, look after yourself." I shouted after her. She smiled and I watched her play with her dog before leaving the park. I found myself doing that a lot, watching people, observing.

Before I met Miss Lancashire, I never really noticed people. I could just walk past someone and take nothing in. But now, I notice everything and everyone because I am curious, because I want to know. If I see someone smile or laugh, I want to know if they had ever been sad. If I see someone sad, I want to know if they have ever been happy. I want to know about their lives, their families, their past – because we all have one. Every day we see so many people. They rush in and out of our lives, and each one's got their own story, their own dreams, their own issues. So many different people all living in the same world, all wanting the same thing. Just to be happy.

    I never thought I would say this but I think Lucy Blackmore was a very lucky girl, she would go home that night to her mum. I used to look down on Lucy during school. I knew she only lived with her mum, and that her mum never worked and always looked scruffy. They lived in a block of flats near the train station, it was not a very nice area. But her mum stood by her with the baby. When it mattered, they were there for each other. And yes, maybe it's really hard for them not having any money, maybe they argue a lot, but they still have each other.

    I did eventually call Miss Lancashire to come and pick me up. She pulled up at the end of my road like she always did. We sat in her car in silence, not really knowing what to say or do for the best. All of a sudden, we heard a loud smash over the car. It was Mum.

    "Oh my God!!" I shouted. Mum had smashed a bottle of wine over the car window. I started to panic because now everyone was going to see us together. Mum was drunk, paralytic. I had never seen her like that before. She looked like a crazy person. She reminded me of Miss Lancashire that night on the hill. Dad was trying to calm her down. Her hands were cut from the broken bottle. Miss Lancashire got out of the car to help. I followed.

    "How could you do this to us you stupid bitch?!" Mum was going for Miss Lancashire with the broken glass from the bottle. Mum must have been drinking all day, she had lost all sense of reality.

    "I know how this must look, but if we can just talk?"

"I don't want you anywhere near me and my family!"

"Mum please." I pleaded.

"Look at you both. What, are you a couple now? It's disgusting!"

"I am helping Maxine find somewhere to stay for the night, she didn't know who else to turn to." Miss Lancashire tried to reason with my parents by telling them anything but the truth.

Some neighbours had come out to see what all the fuss was about. I could see Chloe looking from her bedroom window, curtains were been pulled in other houses. It was chaos. It all seemed so surreal.

"Will you just leave?" Dad shouted at Miss Lancashire as he tried to take Mum back into the house, but she was having none of it.

"Let go of me." She pushed Dad away and stumbled to her car. Mum got her keys from her pocket and got into her car. She turned on the engine. Headlights were on full beam.

"What are you doing Chrissie? You are in no fit state to drive." Dad rushed over, pulling on the car door trying to get in, but she had locked herself in. Mum looked over to me and rolled down the window. She had to shout over the engine.

"You have destroyed this family Maxine."

"Mum please."

In all the commotion – Dad trying to get into the car, me shouting – Mum had started to reverse the car. All of a sudden, we heard a thump. Dad screamed.

"No!" I ran up to the car. Miss Lancashire followed. I looked at my Dad's face and then up to Chloe's bedroom.

She was not there. I walked to the back of the car and Chloe was lying underneath. Mum had run her over. I tried to go to her but Dad was yelling at me to stay away. Miss Lancashire was holding me back. Mum had realised what she had done and became even angrier, yelling and screaming in her car.
"She's not moving! Dad, she's not moving!" I screamed.
"Chloe, Chloe, can you hear me? It's Dad. Chloe, baby, talk to me." There was no response.

Bright lights suddenly came from all directions. The police and ambulance had arrived. A neighbour must have called them when all the shouting started. It was horrendous. The police were trying to get to my mum, the paramedics were trying to help Chloe. After a while, Chloe opened her eyes.

My parents threw me out that night and nothing was ever the same again.

Chapter 24
Peace Of Mind

    Not long after the accident I decided to write a letter to my family.

Dear Mum, Dad and Chloe,

    Where to begin? It feels strange writing you a letter when all I want to do is see you in person and say this to your face. I know you are disgusted with me and don't want to see me again but I love you all. I love you all so much and the thought of never seeing you again breaks my heart.
    I don't know where to start, what to say, how to say it. I never planned it. Sometimes in life, things happen, things that sometimes you just cannot explain or really understand. I hoped at the beginning that we could sit down as a family and talk. I thought you loved me enough for that to happen. But it never did. The hate in your faces when everything happened. I knew you were done with me.
    I am still the same girl though, with the same hopes, dreams and ambition. The same little girl that wants to make you proud, that still needs her Mum and Dad.
    I am sorry for disappointing you, I really am and I know there is nothing I can say that will make you understand.

I want to thank you for the best childhood I could have imagined, for being the best parents. Maybe one day when we are all really old, we can reach out to each other once again. We will all meet up in a nice place, hug each other and be a family again. Or maybe this is really it. The end of us as a family.

I will always be your daughter whatever you think of me now. I will always be proud to call you my Mum and Dad.

I won't give up on you both, even if you have given up on me.

All my love.
Maxine x

P.S. Chloe, I love you, my beautiful little sister. I will always be here for you. If you are ever sad, upset, scared, I want you to look out the window at the sky and I will be doing the same.

Dream big, mini me. Be happy, just be happy xx

I walked to my parents house with the letter one afternoon. It felt strange being on that street again, like I was trespassing. I did not belong there anymore. My parents house looked very different on the outside, almost neglected. There was a big skip in the front, the curtains were drawn in the living room, the plants were overgrown, and there was a *For Sale* sign outside. My dad's car was still in the drive and so I quietly opened the gate and walked up to the front door. I thought about knocking but I knew there was no point, so I gently held open the letter box and pushed my letter through. I hoped so much that my family would read it, that it would make them want to hold me again. But I never heard anything, nothing at all. When I left the house that day, one of the neighbours Maggie pulled into her drive. I stopped and waited until she got out of her car. She saw me and walked into her house, shaking her head. There was no place for me on that street, it was certainly no longer my home.

I also tried to make peace with Lauren and Darcy. I went to Lauren's house a few weeks after posting the letter to my parents. I was nervous walking to her front door. I stood for a few minutes gathering the courage to knock on her door. After a while I did just that. No one answered. I thought about knocking again when the door suddenly opened. It was Lauren's mum, Sharon. She looked shocked to see me.

"Oh, hello Maxine, this is…how are you?"

"I'm okay."

"What can I do for you?"

"I know you don't want me here; I know you must hate me like everyone else, but is Lauren in?"

"Yeah, she is upstairs, wait there. Lauren!" Sharon shouted upstairs to her before turning back to me.

"Look love, I don't hate you, but I do not feel comfortable with you in the house, not after everything that's happened." I nodded trying to hold back the tears. I heard movement from behind her and Lauren came to the door, she was with Darcy. They both looked like they had seen a ghost.

"What do you want?" Lauren stood next to her mum in the doorway.

"Five minutes, please."

"Can we use the garden Mum?" Lauren asked. Darcy did not say anything, she just stared me out. Sharon nodded. Lauren and Darcy came outside and we made our way around the back. We sat at the garden table. It was silent for a while.
"I know you don't want anything more to do with me. I get it."
"How could you?" Darcy snapped.
"I know it's hard to understand."
"You have been sleeping with the head teacher. It's disgusting. Do you know what horrible things people have been saying to us just because we know you? We know about what happened with your family. How do you sleep at night?" Darcy continued. She was really upset with me.
"I didn't come here to argue with you. I know we are done. I just wanted to say sorry for lying to you both and I wanted to say thank you for being my best friends."
We all started to break down, it was too much. I put my hand out on the table longing to reach out to them both. Lauren and Darcy looked at each other. They were hesitant but after a few seconds they put their hands out too. We grasped hands tightly and all sighed with relief. All crying, all knowing how we felt about each other but that it could never go back to how it was. We were best friends; they were my sisters. I loved them. Sharon came round the corner and stood behind Lauren.
"Alright girl's, I think that's enough." We all let go of each other's hands. I got up to leave.
"You won't hear from me again. I love you both so much." I said walking away from them. I could hear them crying. Sharon followed me out.

"Maxine wait." I stopped and turned to her. She held open her arms to me. I was shocked. I did not know what to do.

"It's okay." she said. I walked over to her; she wrapped her arms around me.

"Look after yourself love." I knew I was probably never going to see her again, any of them, and it was the saddest thing. Sharon kissed my forehead and I watched her walk back into her house. That was it. I had my closure.

I quit my A-levels at the end of the first year and unbelievably managed to get B grades across the board in my subjects. I was predicted As but under the circumstances, I was relatively pleased. The qualifications were only worth half of what they could have been, but I could finish them at any time if I wanted to. At a different school or college of course.

Miss Lancashire had left her job too. We had talked about it before she did it and we felt like it was for the best. She told the school board that the stress was too much, the abuse she was getting was starting to take it's toll. She could no longer do her job. There was still an ongoing investigation at that time but at least she was not at school anymore. Miss Lancashire was interviewed by the police after she left but there was never any real proof, nothing that could stand in court. It was all rumours and speculation from teachers and students. I was interviewed too but I never said anything. I never gave anything away despite the police interrogations. Miss Lancashire replaced our phones and destroyed any evidence. I do not know how she did it, she said she would sort it and she did. Everyone knew – the police, family, friends – but there was nothing anyone could do. They were all too late. I was no longer at school and Miss Lancashire was no longer a teacher.

During the time when I had been kicked out and trying to still attend school, I ended up staying with Lucy Blackmore. I know what you're thinking. Who would have thought it? But with the police sniffing around, we could not risk them finding out that Miss Lancashire and I were staying together. So I went to Lucy's flat. I did not know what response I would get from her but when I pressed the door bell, her mum came to the door with nothing but open arms. She helped me, she helped me so much. They did not have much. If I had been into that flat when I was fifteen years old, I would have felt the poorest child ever but at that moment I felt the richest. I felt safe. Lucy and her mum never once asked me if it was true, because to them, it didn't matter. They were just there for me and that's what I needed. It did eventually become common knowledge that the rumours were more than just that. But by that time, no one could prove that our relationship did in fact start in school. They were fighting a losing battle.

What is the perfect family I wonder? In the world you have all kinds of families. Upper class, middle class, working class, lower class. But none of it matters, not really. You can only hope that you are born into a family where you can be yourself and that you are loved for who you are. No matter what you do, no matter what they think. Because you are their child and that should be the most important thing.

It seems that the people in life who have less are the ones that are there for you, because they have nothing to lose. When it came down to it, my family walked away from me. To the outside world, my family looked like the dream, working parents, good kids, nice house, cars, holidays. But I would give up all that to live in a block of flats with nothing, if it meant my parents would have sat down with me and listened. They did not even give me a chance to explain. I guess you don't know how much you mean to someone until it comes down to it. I do think my parents loved me, just not enough. Not in the right way.

Sometimes there comes a time in your life when you just have to let go and move on. Even if it's the hardest thing in the world, even if it makes you feel sick to your stomach. That's what I had to do. I had to let go. But not before I tried one last time. I had waited for a very long time to do this, to see her again, and now that moment was here.

Chapter 25
End Of The Beginning

Present Day – 3.30PM Outside Down Lock Prison

It's still warm. I can feel the heat on my face. It's nice but I have the feeling of sheer panic. I feel overwhelmed, not knowing what to expect, what reaction I will get. I hear a voice from behind me.

"You alright?"

"Yeah thanks, I'm waiting for someone." A man passes me and heads into the reception area of the prison. He looks like security; it wouldn't surprise me around here. It seems to be getting warmer. I look at my watch, time has barely moved. I feel like I have been stood here for hours. I pace about for a few seconds looking around. No one's here. The occasional person catches my attention but they come and go. I knew I would be waiting a bit. I don't have an appointment or anything. It will happen soon though, it needs to.

I look around at the ghetto surroundings. I never thought I would ever be in a place like this. When I think about all the criminals at the other side of this wired fence, I feel upset. She doesn't belong in there with them. She is a good person, genuine and loving. What happened should not have happened and she ended up in a place like this. The building looks cold, separate from the rest of the world.

Before, when I'd walked past it, I was oblivious to the smaller details of the place. Now I have the time I browse the area thoroughly. I walk to a black bin with rubbish over flowing out the sides, writing is scratched into the top. I cannot make it out at first. I think it is a kite with the word *freedom* underneath. I touch it with my hand and can feel the deep indent it has made in the bin. I wonder if a prisoner did this when they were released. Perhaps someone else stood like me waiting and this was their mark, this was their end to a bad situation and now they are free. I smile to myself as a rush of excitement rushes through my body. I suddenly feel a sign of hope that today might go well. When she walks out of here, she will be that kite, she will be free.

I hear some movement from behind the fence. I start to feel sick, like I could pass out at any moment. I hold my clammy hands together. It's time. I can hear footsteps coming in my direction. I can hear her. She is coming, after so long, she is coming. I feel my body go numb. I am so nervous. I do not know what to say or what to do. After a minute or so, the barbed wire fence shakes and a wired gate underneath opens. A policeman walks out, a few seconds pass, and there she is. The person I had not seen for so long. The person I want to hold me and tell me that everything will be okay. I stare at her; she stares at me. I smile at her, tears filling my eyes. She walks a little closer to me. She looks well, all things considering. She is carrying a small bag, wearing casual clothing, top and jeans, hair wrapped in a bun.

I take a deep breath.
"Hello Mum" I say softly. "Hello Mum."

You see the night of the accident; Chloe was badly injured. She did make a full recovery but Mum got sentenced to nearly 18 months in prison for drink driving, accidentally causing harm to a minor and GBH. Mum attacked one of the officers when they were trying to take her down to the station. She cut the policeman's face with a shard of glass. She also had a driving ban for 3 years and had to pay a large fine. Everyone thought her sentencing was harsh but at the time she did not cooperate at all. She just gave up. I tried to see Chloe in the hospital but I was not allowed. I tried to be there for Mum during her sentencing but no one wanted me around. They blamed me for everything. They wanted Miss Lancashire to go to prison but instead it was my mum. They even threatened me with a restraining order if I tried to contact them again. The entire family turned against me. No one understood. No one cared to listen or try to understand. I felt like I had lost everything. But she is still my mum and so today, the day of her release. I am going to try for the very last time to make peace with her.

    I hear a car pull up behind me. I look around and Dad and Chloe get out. Chloe runs to me excited. I hug her so tight.

    "Hey! I have missed you so much." Dad grabs her off me. Chloe looks so grown up. I can't believe how much I have missed out on.

    "We don't want you here." Dad says, not looking at me. Like I am nothing. A waste of space. He takes the bag from Mum and ushers Chloe back into the car. She does not even have time to hug Mum before he sends her away. Mum moves closer to me, she's started crying.

"I want you to listen to me Maxine. You need to leave us alone now." Mum kisses my forehead and walks over to Dad's car.

"Why do you hate me so much?"

"We don't hate you. We love you, but what you did. We gave you everything. How could you? I mean, look at us. Look at what you have done! You ruined this family, and for that we can never forgive you."

"My letter, did you read it?"

"Yes Maxine, I read it. It's over now. We are done."

I watch as my family get into their car and drive away. I watch until I cannot see them anymore, grasping onto every little detail because I know this will probably be the last time I ever see them again. They seem to have made their mind up. I get it. I was their little girl, they had so many hopes and dreams for me and I let them down. I embarrassed them. I can see Chloe in the back seat, putting her hand on the glass. She is crying, screaming my name. I hope that when Chloe is older, she will come and find me and I can be part of her life again. I did not realise at the time but Chloe was the most loyal person in my entire life. Because she knew, she always knew.

I catch my breath and walk a few minutes to the prison car park. I slowly walk to a black BMW. I sit in the passenger seat and slump my shoulders.

"It's over now." I say sinking into my seat. I look over to the driver's seat.

"How was it?" Miss Lancashire is waiting, eager to know. I shake my head.

"You tried darling." Miss Lancashire leans over and kisses me on the cheek. She starts the car and we slowly exit the prison car park. I look out of the window, my eyes full of tears that at any moment are about to drop. What more can I do?

Chapter 26
The Here and Now

My name is Maxine Ann Watts. I am nineteen years old and I live on the outskirts of Manchester with my girlfriend Jane Lancashire, she is thirty nine. After everything started to calm down with the police, we started seeing each other more in public. It wasn't easy, people talking and staring at us all the time. But Manchester is a big place and we started feeling more comfortable when we were out and about. We found our own special places to go to, to visit, to eat at. We knew where we felt safe and normal.

We live in Miss Lancashire's house together. I moved in properly nearly two years ago. We have a dog, a Labrador called Smudge. I work in retail part time, but my ambition is still to work in fashion. I am always drawing and making things. I finish my online fashion course soon and then I might apply for a fashion degree through the *open university*. Not my original education plan but I do believe if I work hard and really try then I can still have my career. Jane works in finance now in the city centre, it's not her passion but she has made some nice friends there and the money is good.

I don't really see anyone anymore, no family or friends. You could say I am alone; it feels like it sometimes. Not by choice, but things are different now.

I still see Lucy– she has a little boy called Max. Sometimes we meet for a coffee or go to the park, occasionally her mum comes along too. It's nice, normal. I never feel judged around them. What I have realised about the Lucy I knew at school was that all she really wanted was to fit in, to belong, to be accepted for who she was. I know better than anyone now how that feels. Maybe we were not so different after all?

    I suppose I did have a path to take, and some think I took the wrong one. That's their opinion, and I'm sure you'll have yours now. That's okay. For the first time in so long I feel at peace with my choices, my decisions, my life. Because after all, this is my life. I never asked for any of this to happen, but it did happen. There is no going back, only forward. I learnt that from Miss Adams. Every day we do things, make decisions, make choices that shape our future and make us the people we are today. I am happy with who I am. I am a good, hard working person, with so much to give this world. My situation started in a place that society deems as wrong. I get that. I see that. I understand. But I knew. I always knew. I knew that it could be something real, if we were given the chance.

    So, there you have it. My story. I've lived it once, said it once and now I end it here today. I do not know what the future holds but I just want to be happy and Jane makes me happy. By reading this and listening to my story, you have done more to try to understand than my parents ever did. And that's even if you finish reading my words and still think that it's wrong, that it's disgusting, that it should never have happened. Even if you think that, if you've got this far, then you have at least tried to understand. And I thank you for that. Because that's all I ever needed – someone who would listen and make an attempt to understand my side.

I do not expect you all to agree and I do not want you to feel sorry for me. I don't want your pity. Maybe you don't, maybe you think I got what I deserved. But it's not about that, I want you to tell people about me. I want you to go to your mum, your dad, your gran, or your best friend – anyone who you are close to, and ask them what they would do if this happened to someone close to them. I want you to ask yourself what you would do if you found yourself in a situation similar to mine. My story is about bringing people together – to talk, to question, to debate.

Mrs Finn once read something to us in English. It was from a book she had come across when she was studying at university.

"Love conquers all. Every cloud has a silver lining. Faith can move mountains. Love will always find a way. Everything happens for a reason. Where there is life, there's hope."

I guess I have always known. The only thing that made any sense, through all the drama, through all the pain, and conflict. I knew that I loved her. I did back then and I do now. I love her more now than I did when this started, and I would never have thought that possible. I cannot explain a feeling to you but there is a reason why everyone wants love so much. I did not understand why until I met Jane Lancashire. It's the closest thing we have to magic.

So, all things considered, after you've taken all this time to try and understand why I did what I did and how I ended up here, let me ask you something.

Is my story about abuse or love?
You can choose your answer now. I already know mine.

Printed in Great Britain
by Amazon